Real or Magic?

Kari Stokely
Illustrated by Rosabel Rosalind

Real or Magic?

Copyright © 2020 by Kari Stokely. All rights reserved.

No part of this book may be reproduced or transmitted in any form or by any means, electronic or mechanical, including photocopying, recording, or by any information storage and retrieval system, without the express written permission of the author.

ISBN-13: 978-1-7355785-0-7

www.529bookdesign.com
Cover art: Rosabel Rosalind
Cover: Claire Moore
Interior: Lauren Michelle

Real
or
Magic?

KARI STOKELY

Contents

1. The Dark Side of the Moon   1
2. Real or Magic?   5
3. Do Not Enter   13
4. Legends and Lore   17
5. Inside the Potting Shed   28
6. The Other Side of the Potting Shed   33
7. Wild Bear Woods   38
8. The Girl from the Prophecy   43
9. 43 Degrees North, 2 Degrees East   54
10. Back in the Potting Shed   60
11. Little River Cave   68
12. Hoppy!   73
13. The Full Moon   80
14. Hanging on by a Thread   82
15. The Killing Ceremony   90
16. Stella's Observatory   96
17. The Demon Inside   103

18 The Beginning of Time   109

19 The Time Traveler's Code   119

20 The Great Stone Shelf   125

21 The Medicine Man   129

22 Math Class   133

23 The Great Escape   136

24 The White Doe   143

25 A Dance with the Wintry Wind   149

26 Time Is Time   151

27 Great Stag Forest   155

28 Poof!   157

29 The Little Note   159

30 O' Sweet Freedom   161

31 Magic Tools: Distraction and Deception   167

32 Grandpa Doc   180

33 The Battle   184

34 Time Expired   190

Real
or
Magic?

FIFTY MILLION YEARS AGO, after dinosaurs became extinct but long before humans walked the Earth, the mighty Mystic River raged through the mountains of Southwest Europe. It carved steep cliffs, jutting shelves, winding ledges, enormous canyons, and intricate caves along its way. For forty-eight million years, the rapid waters flowed. Then, two million years ago, the Earth became very cold, snow replaced rain, and massive ice sheets formed. As water became ice, the Mystic River receded, but the cliffs, shelves, ledges, canyons, and caves all remained.

FIFTY THOUSAND YEARS AGO, when the North Pole's ice cap covered much of Europe, a small community of humans lived in a vast cave alongside a wide ledge that had been sculpted into the mountainside by the Mystic River. They called the ledge the Great Stone Shelf. It was a gathering place for good—and evil.

PRESENT DAY….

1
THE DARK SIDE OF THE MOON

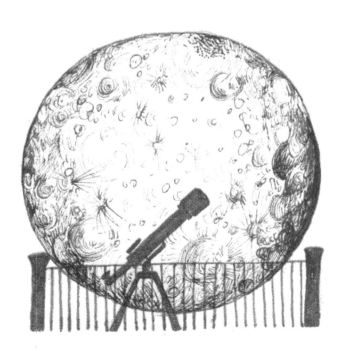

Québec City, Canada
Wintertime

"HELLO, MOON. WHY DON'T you show me your dark side for once?" Sky begged playfully. From the flat roof of her little rowhouse, she peered through her telescope, scanning the craters Tycho and Copernicus. "I don't see any unidentified flying objects on your surface tonight." With her red-gloved hand, she made a note in her notebook and then clicked RECORD on her cell phone. "February tenth. There is only one new shadow. It's in the Moon's Sea of Serenity."

The door of the roof-access hut creaked. "Hi, Sky. It's freezing up here," her mama said, cinching her parka hood to her face. "What are you looking at tonight?"

"The Moon—trying to convince it to show me its dark side. Hey, Papa, we're working on our spaceship and learning about Ursa Major this weekend, right?"

"Absolutely. We're gonna have a great view of the constellation from the farm—no light pollution out there."

"Are we going to Grandpa Doc's? I can't believe he moved to that creepy, old farm when he retired."

"It's not creepy. It's the house he grew up in. He loves it there." Papa took a deep breath and braced himself. "Sky, we're movin' to the farm, too. Hope and I lost our jobs."

The telescope nearly fell off the tripod as Sky spun around. "What? You're kidding, right? You expect me to leave my friends and just go live on a stupid farm in the middle of nowhere? I'll die of boredom. And, what about my birthday party next month?" A tear fell from her eye. "You're a policeman, and Hope is a police dog...there must be lots of jobs."

An icy breeze sliced the air between Sky and her parents, ruffling the pages of her notebook.

"We're startin' a simpler life. We're movin' Saturday."

"Saturday! It's the middle of the school year. Are you crazy?"

"We're going to homeschool you."

"Great! Now, I'll have no friends and be stupid. You're ruining my life." Sky shoved her notebook and cell phone in her backpack with her binoculars and survival kit. She grabbed her telescope, stormed past her parents, and slammed the rooftop door. Then, she opened it again. "I'm not going!" She glared at them. "You're the worst parents in the world. I hate you." Tears streamed from her eyes as she slammed the door again.

Before her parents could respond, Sky flew down the spiral staircase, ran to her room, and slammed her bedroom door. She dumped the contents of her backpack, then picked up her notebook and scribbled something in it. She ripped the page out and taped it to the outside of her door: *I'M NOT GOING!*

Back on the icy-cold rooftop, Mama and Papa stared at each other, unsure of what to say.

LATER THAT NIGHT, SKY slid a note under her parents' bedroom door that read: *I'm not going! I'll live with Grandma and Grandpa Montagne if I must. I'm not leaving my friends or my school. Have a good life without me!*

She whistled for Hope. As she held the dog tight, she whispered, "I'm not going to the farm...no matter what."

2
REAL OR MAGIC?

ON SATURDAY AFTERNOON, SKY stared out the window as Papa stopped the old, red truck at the end of a country lane in front of a big, white farmhouse. She had only been to her great-grandparents' farm once—when she was a baby.

Grandpa Doc watched the truck come to a stop on the snowy lane. "Hello, Sky. Let's hurry up and get inside. It's freezing out here." He grabbed her suitcase and the box filled with her prized possessions.

They took the back staircase up. At the top, there was a long, wide hallway with wild animal heads mounted to the walls.

Sky startled on seeing the great creatures.

"I'm sorry," Grandpa Doc said, "I didn't mean for those to scare you. I should've warned you."

"They don't scare me. They surprised me. Did you…kill them with your bow?"

"No, before I could retire to the farm, a caretaker lived here. He left them. Your dad and I will take them down."

She studied the animals for a long moment. "It looks like the stag wants to fight the bear."

"I'm not sure who would win that battle."

Sky remembered she was in the middle of her own battle and withdrew from the conversation with a shrug.

"The yellow-checkered-window room will be yours," Grandpa Doc said, leading her down the hallway.

The room was a large nook with a ceiling that soared into a peak to accommodate an oversized window. The window was made of yellow and clear glass panes, laid out like a checkerboard. Below it was a large window seat with built-in drawers at both ends. On top of the window seat was a mattress covered with a colorful patchwork quilt. Beautiful crystal knobs ran diagonally up the two walls of the window nook.

Sky dropped her winter gear and backpack by the door and plopped herself on the bed. She pulled her legs to her chest, wrapped her arms around them, and stared out one of the clear windowpanes.

"You can hook the quilt loops on the glass knobs to create a tent—like sleeping under the stars." Grandpa Doc took her books, collection of discarded cell phones, and stuffed animals out of the box and placed them above the drawers, next to the extra handmade quilts. He picked Hoppy up again.

He ran his finger along the green stitching where Hoppy—Sky's favorite stuffed animal—once had a tail, then he ran it along the yellow stitching where the leg had been reattached. "Life is full of battles. Do you remember the day we rescued Hoppy from the dusty, old box on the top shelf of Ye Olde Antique Shoppe?" Grandpa Doc said, remembering the battle between the puppy Hope and brand-new Hoppy. He touched Hoppy's beautifully quilted ear—the ear that had been stitched to the bunny's head with purple thread that day. "Often, actually more often than not, something wonderful emerges from the battle—something that would have never happened otherwise."

He put the stuffed animal down, unrolled Sky's world map, and taped it to the wall above her bed. Then, he put the telescope case in one corner of the room and the bow case in another. "Tomorrow won't be as cold—sunny with no wind. In the afternoon, we'll set up the targets and practice a little. And tomorrow night, I'll show you Stella's observatory," Grandpa Doc said, hoping he had pulled at two of Sky's heartstrings. "Stella was my mom and your great-grandma."

Sky shrugged and continued to look out the window. Through a gap in the row of evergreen trees, she saw an ornate spire on a metal roof.

Grandpa Doc snapped his fingers. As Sky turned to look, he pulled a coin out of her ear and flicked it into a fast, spinning motion. The spinning coin transformed into a snow globe, glistening with tiny galaxies made up of teeny-tiny stars and planets.

"Real or magic, Sky?"

Sky smiled. Then, *poof!* The miniature universe was gone. Her smile vanished along with it. She looked back out the window again.

Grandpa Doc looked at his watch, adjusting the face. "Dinner will be in an hour."

Sky turned to answer her grandfather a moment too late.

Poof!

He was gone.

"Hoppy, we need to learn to disappear. Come on, let's get out of here." She put on her winter gear and backpack, grabbed Hoppy, and closed her bedroom door. "Everyone's in the kitchen. We'll take the front staircase," she whispered to her trusted, furry friend.

Halfway down the staircase, she crouched, grabbed two spindles, and peered between them. "Hoppy, we're prisoners, stuck behind these prison bars." At that moment, she noticed the prison bars weren't cold, smooth metal. They were intricately carved wooden spindles, like little totem poles—some with animals and others with geometric designs. "Are you an African elephant or an Asian elephant?" she whispered to the elephant on the mahogany spindle. "I see you're all alone, too. I bet you were taken from your friends and everything you love."

Hoppy whispered, "At least you weren't taken from me. I can't imagine life without you."

"Oh, Hoppy, I'll never let anyone take you from me," Sky said as she tucked Hoppy into the side pocket of her backpack.

A few minutes later, they slipped out the front door and down the country lane.

3

DO NOT ENTER

"HOPPY, THERE'S THE BREAK in the trees." Sky trudged through the snow to the building with the ornate spire.

Except for the roof, the fancy shed was completely covered with a dense, thorny thicket. Through the shrubbery, she could see it was made of tightly stacked, finely cut, heavy stone. One side had a massive oak door flanked by two fancy windows. Each of the other sides had a large window. The thick planks of the door were reinforced with two ancient, hand-forged, iron braces. The door had a large, metal handle, and a sign covered with graffiti. Both the sign and the graffiti read: *Do Not Enter.*

"I need a place to hide," Sky said, struggling with the vines that had latched themselves to the stone. "Come on, let go." She tugged at the vine that covered the door. "If I didn't know better, I'd think you were trying to hide something." She squatted, grabbing the base of the vine. With all her might, she yanked it. As the vine let go of its hold, she was tossed to the ground.

Whoosh!

"Geez!" Sky said, as she landed on her side and slid across the snow. When she finally came to a stop, she rolled onto her stomach and swiped away the snow. "Hoppy, it's a frozen stream." She stood up, brushed herself off, and tiptoed off the ice and back to the fancy shed.

She ran a gloved hand over the massive cold stone and foreboding oak door. She took a step back and put both hands on her hips. In her best King's English accent, she interrogated the building. "What yu' think yu' are with yur stone walls—a castle? What yu' protectin'? A king? A queen? A princess?" She peered into a window but couldn't see anything. "Yu' must be protectin' somethin' so I'll need me a sword." She picked up a long, pointed stick.

Sky stepped back and studied the castle and its frozen moat. Suddenly, she felt the ground shake.

Crack!

The ice shattered, like glass.

"Do you see that, Hoppy?" She readied her sword.

Crash!

A golden-horned dragon smashed through the ice. It roared a mighty roar and extended its deadly claws.

Sky lunged at the dragon. Then, it disappeared beneath the ice-covered moat.

"Jiminy Cricket. Did you see that, Hoppy?"

Hoppy shivered. "That was a huge dragon!"

"Oh, silly rabbit, it was tiny…like a small dog."

Sky scanned the broken ice but couldn't see the dragon anywhere, so she turned her attention to the castle. "If yu' are a castle, yu' must be fortified with a portcullis to defend against intruders who crossed yur moat and slayed yur dragon." She looked up to see if there was an iron gate with pointed ends that could be rolled down by the guards inside to spear and trap the enemy.

"Your signs, dragon, and ancient door don't scare me." She wrestled with the handle on the door, but it wouldn't budge. She grew tired of attacking the castle and slaying the dragon, so she tossed her sword on the ground. She pressed her body weight into the door, turned the handle with all her might, and said, "Come on, *door...unlock.*"

The door flew open, and Sky went tumbling in.

4

LEGENDS AND LORE

The Great Stone Shelf, Southwest Europe
Fifty Thousand Years Ago

LUNE HEARD THE CRUSHING, rhythmic beating of the Powerful Ones' spears against the Great Stone Shelf. It was the sound of the Killing Ceremony—a sound that meant a Tainted One was being bound with leather rope to be left for dead in Wild Bear Woods.

The teenager—cloaked from head to toe in the furs of a white doe—held back tears as she looked first at her father, Okeanos, and then at the Medicine Man. *Why is it this way?* she signed, not wanting to be overheard.

Angry, Okeanos gestured, *The Powerful Ones kill us to make us fear them...to keep us oppressed.* His eyes narrowed as he cinched the furs of a black bear to his waist.

Lune shook her head. *It's not right, Father.* Then, she turned to the Medicine Man, searching for answers.

From behind his gray wolf mask, the Medicine Man leaned on his crystal-topped staff, studying Lune's question. Finally, he growled, not caring if the Powerful Ones overheard him. "Loch is sick." Then, he departed, reluctantly taking his required place on the Great Stone Shelf next to Loch—king of the Powerful Ones, persecutor of the Tainted Ones.

Lune and Okeanos pulled their hoods over their heads, masking their faces. With the other Tainted Ones, they walked through the cave chambers and onto the Great Stone Shelf.

As the Tainted Ones entered the Great Stone Shelf, a masked guard snorted, "Women and children, kneel down there...men, to the jail." Each guard was clothed in the furry, dead flesh of wild boars—from the tip of the long, black snout to the curly pig tail, and with all the tusks and hooves in between.

When it was time for Lune and Okeanos to be sorted, the guard lowered his eyes, regretting what he was about to say. "You two...up there."

Lune gasped. "Father, the guard is sending us up front. That means Trasnet and Tunet must be the accused." She looked at the accused—who had been forced to remove their masks—and immediately recognized her brothers.

Infuriated, Okeanos shook his head at the thought of killing one of his adopted sons. *Hold your head high,* he gestured to Lune as they took their place behind the teenage boys.

A few minutes later, Loch made his grand entrance. He marched onto the Great Stone Shelf and took his place, front and center. He was gowned in the furs of a mighty stag—from the crown of antlers that masked his head to the hooves that clanked and dangled at his wrists and ankles. To Loch's right stood the Medicine Man—the Great Gray Wolf.

From behind her mask, Lune glared at Loch. Before Loch could turn the heavy antlers around to smirk at her, she turned her stone-cold gaze to the crowd. From the corner of her eye, she could see the guards all around—beating their spears against the ground in one hand while holding a long, thin, leather rope in the other as a threat to anyone who might rebel, as if the wooden spears tipped with sharp stone weren't enough.

When the Tainted Ones were sorted, Loch raised his ancient ceremonial spear high, and the rhythmic beating stopped. He puffed out his thick chest and roared:

"Lore and legend, tales of old,
A Tall Tribe girl, that's what's told.
This one, you say, she's the one...
Who frees the tarnished, the Tainted Ones.
You say she possesses flying spears,
And controls the animals far and near.
You say she'll hold the sun in her hand.
Hah! You think she'll free you from this land?
Your legends and lore are mere hoopla.
Your myths will be your tragic flaw."

Loch paused for a moment, raising his eyes to the Moon, casting the shadows of his antlers throughout the Great Stone Shelf.

Loch's emotions ebbed and flowed with the Moon. For five days each month, just as the Moon turned full, he'd turn into a complete and utter lunatic, bringing terror to those he ruled. Then, he'd grow calm again—with no memory of the terror he had inflicted, or so it seemed.

Loch snapped his head down, thrusting his antlers and spear at the jailed men. He cocked his head from one side to the other, sneering from under his mask. "Hogwash and lies, the myths you were told...the Tall Tribe are cunning and weak but never bold."

He whipped around, pointing his spear high in the air and his fist toward the accused. "No one like the Prophecy

Girl exists!" Loch let out a sinister howl that echoed over the rocky shelf, down the northeast ledge, and into Great Stag Forest—his kingdom to the east. "And, if, by some twist, she suddenly appears...I promise I'll hunt her without any fear. I'll find her and bind her and leave her for dead. Oh, such bloodshed to hang over your heads!"

As Lune fought tears, she thought, *I won't let him kill my brother.* She squashed her tears as Loch yelled:

"You, the Tainted Ones, mixed of Powerful and Tall,
This is the law, so hear it all.
Tunet stole a spear, so his brother, Trasnet, must die.
We'll leave him for the lioness until we hear his last cry.
A cry like all cries before...
Let it haunt Tunet and his people forevermore!"

Lune devised a plan as she watched the Powerful Ones hold their spears high and chant, "Long live the Powerful Ones!"

When the crowd finally quieted down, Loch turned to Tunet. "Tie the last knot, Tunet!"

"No," Tunet said, firmly. "I returned my spear to the Powerful Ones' vault. One of yours planted it in my chamber."

Loch's twisted thoughts and sick emotions coiled within him as he heard the Full Moon jeer, "I control you just like I control the great tidal waves of the seas. Teach him who's boss!"

Loch threw a punch that landed square in Tunet's gut.

The Full Moon sneered at Loch, "If you want to control the Tainted Ones, show their leader, Okeanos, who's in control. Threaten him and Tunet with the girl."

Loch's anger turned to rage as he glared at Tunet. He threatened, "Tie the knot without further ado, or Lune, the White Doe, will die too."

Trasnet looked at Tunet and nodded. The brothers locked eyes one last time. Tunet's eyes filled with tears as he knelt and tied the final knot in the thin, leather rope.

Loch screamed, "Guards, loosen the boulders and slide the prison's gate. Lock up Tunet and Okeanos with the other Tainted men while Trasnet meets his fate." He scanned the edge of the shelf where a hollow in the mountain wall served as a prison—latticed logs bound by sinew served as prison bars.

Loch glared at Okeanos and Tunet as they embraced Trasnet one last time and then watched them enter the jail. He turned to his guards and commanded:

"Guards, make sure you have them all!
Count the Tainted Ones, mixed of Powerful and Tall.
One, two, three, four, five, six, seven...
There's another four so, in total, eleven.

Always be counting, again and again.
Within the jail, eleven must remain."

Loch placed the tip of his ancient ceremonial spear in one of the roaring fires.

The fires' golden embers flicked into the air, taunting a massive block of ice in the Sacred Stone Water Basin, daring it to transform into water in the frozen, arctic world. If it were not for the fire and the ice, there would be no water for the people.

Once the spear's tip was hot, Loch dragged it across Trasnet's cheek. "If the lioness doesn't make the kill, then the buzzards most certainly will." He paused, staring at the bloody, burnt cut. "Now, it's time for the Medicine Man to curse this boy. Come, sprinkle devil dust here and there. Joy, oh, joy."

But the Medicine Man never stepped forward, throwing Loch into a fit of rage. Loch's eyes bulged from his mask and his hand choked the spear as he bellowed:

"Where's the Great Gray Wolf, that old Medicine Man?
He's always wandering about when I need him at hand.
We'll just skip the formalities
And get on with the brutalities.
For three suns, count them: one, two, three,
The Tainted Ones will be kept under lock and key.
Tainted women and children: Get to your cave
And don't you dare leave 'til you're told.
Lest you wish great, bloody havoc to unfold."

Lune looked straight at Loch as he directed his rage to her. "You first, get into your chamber, Tainted girl."

Lune's blood boiled. She hated that the Powerful Ones called them "Tainted" Ones. *People are people, even if they have both Tall Tribe and Powerful One ancestry,* she thought. She put her emotions aside and held her head high as she walked past the guards who stood at the entrance to the Tainted Ones' main cave. She walked through several chambers and then entered a crevice—her tiny bedroom. In the distance, she could still hear Loch:

"Guarders of the Tainted:
Here's how we'll keep them isolated.
Some take your stance at the Tainted cave's entrance.
Others stand ready and do not fail
To keep the Tainted men in our jail.
Give them food and water but not a lot...
We will teach them a lesson but not let them rot.

Bearers of the Body:
First, gag the boy so that there's nothing he can say.
Next, mask him for his final day.
Then, lift the bounded, tarnished, tainted Trasnet.
And leave him for dead—for his deepest, darkest day.

Holders of the Fire, listen as I inspire:
To Wild Bear Woods—lead the way.
Trek down the southwest ledge without delay.
Cross the meadow that's drifted with snow and ice.
There, leave Trasnet for dead without thinking twice."

Inside the comfort of her tiny room, Lune stopped listening. She pushed off the white doe head that masked her face and crawled into a hidden passageway that extended deep into the mountain. She followed it to her secret cave, where she kept her prized possessions. There, she grabbed two spears, a knife, dried meat, and medicinal herbs. From the great underground cave, she took the passageway that snaked its way to the base of the mountain and narrowed to the tiniest of exits. She reached back and pulled her hood over her head and onto her face—the White Doe slipped into the frigid, night air.

Sleeker than the lioness, Lune crossed the Icy Meadow and hid deep in Wild Bear Woods behind a dense tree. From her hiding place, she spied two things: the Tree That Was Never There and four guards carrying Trasnet down the mountain's southwest ledge.

5

INSIDE THE POTTING SHED

"GEEZ!" SKY STOOD UP, brushed herself off, and got her flashlight just before a cold wind slammed the old, oak door shut.

She shined her flashlight around the dusty room. The walls, floor, and ceiling were made of a shiny, albeit dusty, metal. "That's weird. I was expecting stone walls. Look, Hoppy, we can see everything outside."

Hoppy shivered. "It's kind of creepy in here."

"Oh, Hoppy, don't worry. I'll protect you," Sky said, squeezing the bunny.

"The inside is definitely not part of the castle. It has the same windows as the castle but no door in the doorway."

She pressed Hoppy's face between the two walls. "And look, you can see the dust and dirt between the metal wall and the castle wall—two separate buildings. How weird is that?"

She shined the flashlight around the room. "There's not much of anything in here except some shelves. And look at that…what a strange candlestick."

"It's not a candlestick. It's an antique phone. It's so old that I only ever saw one for sale at Ye Olde Antique Shoppe."

"It only has one number, zero. Let's pretend to call Grandma Montagne."

As she dialed, a metal door behind her slid quietly into place, locking her in.

"Hello, I'd like to call Grandma Montagne or any of my great-grandmothers," Sky said playfully.

To Sky's surprise, a voice said, "This is operator five-one-zero-three-seven. I'm placing the first call to Lune at destination coordinates 43 degrees north, 2 degrees east. Please hold while I confirm a connection."

Before Sky could say anything, a second operator responded, "*Bonjour, c'est l'opérateur quatre-deux-huit-six-zéro. Vous êtes connecté.*"

Sky was amazed to hear a second operator, and one speaking French, no less.

"You have thirty seconds to deposit five cents for a five-minute connection. The potting shed will return to the origin when time expires," the first operator said.

"But Grandma lives—"

"Lune is at destination coordinates 43 degrees north, 2 degrees east. You have fifteen seconds remaining to make the deposit."

The conversation was so quick and direct that Sky did what the operator said.

Beside the phone, she noticed two jars. The first jar was filled with nickels. The second jar had a slotted lid and a label that read *Deposit*. She took a nickel from the first jar and put it in the second jar.

The operator warned, "At the destination, open and close the metal door using the commands *Open Door* and *Close Door*. At the origin, lock and unlock the oak door using the commands *Door Unlock* and *Door Lock*. When you're outside, keep the door closed. Please take a watch from the watch box. Your five-minute call will end when the time expires."

"Wow, voice-activated doors...that's pretty fancy technology for an old castle!" Sky shined her flashlight and saw a box labeled *Watch Box*.

She picked a watch and noticed how beautiful it was. The face was a sixty-second stopwatch with one elaborate hand and beautifully scripted markers. The marker at the top read *Time Expired*. Within the face of the watch, there were two tiny compasses, one with *N*, *S*, *E*, and *W*, and the other with only two words where the N should be—*Potting Shed*. The watch did not have a crown—the knob used to set the time.

Sky looked at Hoppy. "It's pointing to the five. But why would we need a watch?"

Hoppy shrugged. "I don't know. Maybe so we know when the five-minute call is over?"

The old phone went dead.

They both stared at it for a bit.

"That's so weird, Hoppy. She just hung up on us."

"This is really creepy, Sky."

"Let's get out of here." She turned to leave. "Jiminy Cricket, where's the door?" Panic ran through Sky's body and sweat beaded on her face. "It has to be over here." She shined her flashlight on the dusty metal wall with the two fancy windows. "I'm sure it was there." Just then, she saw an outline of a door and pressed her body against it, but it wouldn't budge.

"Oh, no, here we go again with this stupid, old door. What was the command? Oh, yeah…unlock door!"

Nothing happened.

"*Door Unlock.*"

Sky pressed her body weight against the metal wall. "Stupid door, open up." She gave the door a little kick. "I remember. *Open Door.*"

And, just like that, the metal door slid open.

6

THE OTHER SIDE OF THE POTTING SHED

SKY STEPPED OUT OF the potting shed and into the bitter cold, clutching Hoppy in her arms.

"Wow, look at this. We're not on the farm anymore. There's not just a row of evergreen trees, there's a whole forest of them! And look at that icy meadow and snow-covered mountain. It's twice as big as the ones at home. It sure would be fun to sled down that mountain and through the meadow's snow-drifted paths." Sky unclipped the bear spray from her backpack just as an icy wind smacked her in the face, stole her breath, snatched Hoppy into the air, and tossed him on the ground.

"Hoppy!" She ran, scooped him up, and held him tight while she pulled the drawstrings on her parka hood.

Hoppy shivered. "That was scary."

"I have a great idea." Sky twirled around and then threw Hoppy high in the air where, once again, he was caught in a gust of wind. She chased after him and grabbed him just as he was about to slide down an ice drift. "Tomorrow, we're taking the potting shed to see Daisy Riverstone in the city. This is way cooler than a video chat."

She turned back around to see the woods but choked on her words. "Where's the potting shed? I can't see it. Where is it?"

As she caught her breath and ran back, she saw the open door and the dusty inside of the potting shed. She scolded the potting shed, "Jiminy Cricket, don't do that to me!"

Sky scrunched up her face as she inspected the exterior walls. "Where are the castle walls? I can feel the metal walls. Only the metal building is here, but it looks like a tree—it's pretending to be a tree. Now I know how those shadows on the Moon appear! They're UFOs like this—blending into their surroundings, like a chameleon, and casting their shadow onto the ground. We're probably in a faraway galaxy."

They walked around the magical tree and pressed their faces against it where the windows should be.

"Look, Hoppy, you can't see inside at all. This is so awesome. We have our own UFO." She twirled around, threw Hoppy in the air, and caught him on his way down. "Did you feel that, Hoppy? I just felt a snowflake. It's snowing!" She aimed his face toward the sky.

After catching snowflakes on their tongues, they walked back into the dusty room and commanded the metal door to close.

"Look, you can see out, just like at home. Hoppy, you stand in here and point the light at this window. I just want to be sure that no one—especially Mama and Papa—will ever know we're in here." She helped the bunny to the shelf and handed him the flashlight.

The flashlight dropped.

"You're shaking, Hoppy. Are you cold?"

"No, I'm frightened. You're coming right back, right?" Hoppy pressed the flashlight button twice to put it in strobe-light mode.

"Yes, I'll be right back, don't worry. This is going to be fun!" Sky touched MUSIC on her cell phone, selected her funkiest playlist, touched PLAY, turned up the volume, and commanded the door to open and then close. She walked all around the UFO and didn't see or hear Hoppy's wild and crazy party inside. All she heard was icy, wintry silence.

"Hoppy, it's soundproof, and I couldn't see any light at all."

She practiced the door commands and then took her notebook out of her backpack and scribbled the commands on three sheets of paper. She ripped two pages out, tucking one under the deposit jar and the other in her parka pocket.

Then, she touched RECORD on her cell phone. "Hoppy, if I've said it once, I've said it a million times—we always need a backup system. Using just paper will never do." She recorded everything she could remember about the call with the operator and then renamed the recording to OPERATOR.

Sky checked the watch—the hand had barely moved. She looked into the bunny's eyes. "I wonder how long we're going to be here. The operator said it was going to be a five-minute call, but we've been here at least a half hour." Her stomach growled as she stared out the windows.

The sky was growing dark when a shimmer caught her eye. She ran from window to window but saw nothing—just evergreens and snowdrifts. "I'm so hungry that I'm starting to see things, Hoppy."

She pressed her face against the window and surveyed the Moon. "We're not in a faraway galaxy, Hoppy. We're on Earth. The Moon is rising in the east and has the same craters and seas as our Moon. Maybe, our UFO is superfast, and we're in Siberia or Alaska! I doubt we're in Antarctica because I don't think there are woods there."

At least another half hour passed when Sky saw torches coming down the mountainside. "Do you see those people carrying torches?"

Hoppy trembled as he peered out the window.

"They're coming this way, and…they're carrying something." She gripped the bear spray in her hand as she looked at the watch.

For the first time since she walked out the front door of the farmhouse, Sky wished she were in the colorful tent under the yellow-checkered window, safe and sound in her new bedroom—sleeping under the stars.

7

WILD BEAR WOODS

FROM INSIDE THE UFO, Sky watched the men march past her and into the woods. "Hoppy, they look really creepy, wearing those black pig heads and all. Look at the tusks sticking out of their faces."

Hoppy shivered. "Those are the skins of a wild boar."

"They're carrying a boy…he's all tied up…he's not dead…I saw him move. Jiminy Cricket, they put him on the ground, and they're leaving him in the middle of the woods. And now they're marching back through the icy meadow and up the mountain. Hoppy, I'll be right back." Sky opened her survival kit, slipped her pocketknife and scissors into her parka pocket, grabbed the bear spray, and commanded the door to open and then close.

FROM HER HIDING PLACE in the woods, Lune watched the guards deposit Trasnet on a rock and then leave. Without a sound, she moved to his side and quickly untied the loose knot in the leather rope that gagged him.

"Lune, what are you doing here? Go home or Loch will kill you too," Trasnet commanded.

"I won't let my brother die. Shh—" She tried to untie the knots in the leather strips that bound his body to his limbs, but there were too many, and, except for the knot that Tunet tied, they were all very tight. She sawed at the straps with her stone knife.

On hearing an unusual sound, not a winter squirrel or a night owl but that of an intruder, Lune sprang to her feet and drew her spear, ready to strike.

Surprised, Sky jumped back and held her hands high in the air. "I'm here to help!"

Lune assessed the unarmed girl. *She's from the Tall Tribe.*

"Please, let me help," Sky pleaded.

Snap!

Crunch!

Both girls turned. In the distance, they heard the forest floor rustle with the snapping of dried twigs and the crunching of dried leaves. The noise drew nearer.

"I wish I had my bow," Sky said to herself, holding the bear spray as if it were a gun. She moved toward the sound and then waited.

The shadow of a massive figure stepped from behind the trees—assessing its prey, clearly wanting a fight. From under its breath and powerful jowl, there came a treacherous, frightening growl. It curled the deadly nails of its paws and let out a deep roar with the snap of its jaw.

Lune knelt and whispered, "Trasnet, scream so Loch thinks you're dead and the bear knows you're human." She stood back up and drew her spear.

"No!" Trasnet screamed.

The bear flared its nostrils and its snout opened wide as it looked up to the heavens, thrashing its head from side to side. From the depth of its lungs, it released a second deafening roar. To the ground it went, and from there, the mighty omnivore charged the kids.

Sky pointed the can at the bear's face and gave it a blast, hoping the loud noise would scare it from afar.

The bear continued to charge—dodging fallen trees here and there—quickly reducing the distance.

"I can't see it," Sky said as she peered everywhere and forced herself to stay calm. She aimed toward where she'd imagined the bear's nose to be and sprayed in a zigzag.

The peppery barrier seeped into the bear's nasal passages, ears, and eyes—stinging it, scaring it, forcing it to retreat just in the nick of time.

Sky leaned down and helped Lune finish cutting the leather straps that bound Trasnet's limbs to his body. As they helped him up, Sky said, "Hurry, let's go."

Lune and Trasnet followed Sky to the Tree That Was Never There.

"*Open Door,*" Sky commanded the metal door to open.

They dodged inside.

"*Close Door,*" Sky said.

And the door sealed shut behind them.

8

THE GIRL FROM THE PROPHECY

"YOU CAN TELL ME what the heck was going on out there another day. But right now, I need to take care of that gross gash on your face. Blood is oozing from under that brown deer ski mask of yours. GR-ross." Sky scrunched her nose and looked deep into Trasnet's eyes. "Don't worry, my grandpa is a surgeon. He taught me everything I need to know to stitch you up."

Trasnet stared at Sky for a moment and then gestured, *She's the girl from the prophecy. She's from the Tall Tribe.*

Lune signed, *She controlled the bear.*

"I know you're talking about me and the bear." Sky mimicked Lune's scratching in the air, like bears do. "As soon as I'm finished with surgery, you can teach me some words, so we can talk to each other."

Sky pointed to herself and said, "Sky."

Lune and Trasnet understood and introduced themselves.

"Silly me, I forgot to introduce Hoppy." Sky helped Hoppy off the dusty shelf. "He has a bad leg, but that doesn't get him down. He just needs a little help sometimes. Grandpa Doc and I stitched Hoppy's leg on when he lost it. It was gross, too. Blood was oozing everywhere!"

Hoppy looked into Lune's eyes and did a little bow as Sky introduced him. "Hoppy, Lune—Lune, Hoppy." Then Hoppy turned to Trasnet and bowed as Sky introduced them. "Hoppy, Trasnet—Trasnet, Hoppy."

Trasnet returned the bow to the little bunny.

"Trasnet, I need you to remove your mask. It's in the way of my surgery." Sky untied her hood and pushed it down, gesturing for him to do the same. She turned to Lune and said, "You too, so I can see your face."

Sky became serious as she looked deep into Trasnet's eyes. "Someone cut you and burned you." She pointed at his wound. "Your body is in a battle right now—microscopic warriors called white blood cells are battling the germs that infiltrated your body. And don't let their size fool you. Microscopic organisms are powerful! If the white blood cells don't win the battle, you'll get sick." She shook her head. "And, you don't want to get sick." She pretended to throw up. "I hate throwing up. Anyway, I need to help the warriors win. Okay?"

Trasnet nodded. He didn't understand the words she was saying, yet he somehow understood their meaning.

Sky took the scissors and pocketknife out of her pocket and examined them.

Trasnet's eyes opened wide.

"Don't worry, I won't have to use my knife," Sky said as she opened an alcohol wipe and put on disposable surgical gloves. "A magnifying glass and tweezers will do the trick." She cleaned the knife and scissors and put them away.

"Hoppy, show Trasnet that everything will be okay—show him all your battle wounds."

Trasnet signed jokingly, *Do you think I'm getting purple stitching, Lune?*

"I know what you're signing, and, no, I don't have any green thread. Bandages will have to do. And, yes, you will have a big scar, like Hoppy's. As my Grandpa Doc says: Out of most battles, something wonderful happens that would have never happened otherwise. Just look at Hoppy, for example. He would've never had his beautiful, colorful ear if he hadn't stood up for himself and battled the puppy Hope on his first day at home. Right, Hoppy?"

Lune snorted as she laughed at how talkative Sky was.

Sky picked up the flashlight and shined it on Trasnet's wound.

Lune and Trasnet's eyes both grew wide.

She holds the sun in her hand, Lune signed, *just like the Prophecy Girl.*

Sky knew Lune was talking about the flashlight and shined it on Lune's face for a split second, smiling before turning it back to study Trasnet's wound. She picked up the magnifying glass. "Lune, I need an assistant. Please hold the light for me." She put the flashlight in Lune's hand.

Trasnet signed, *Look who holds the sun in her hand now. Maybe you're the Tall Tribe girl in the prophecy—maybe you're the Prophecy Girl.*

Lune laughed. *I'm only part Tall Tribe. Besides, I didn't control the bear.*

It was easy to learn the word for bear, as Lune made a scary bear face, growled, and scratched the air.

"You'll have to tell me about the bear later," Sky said, adjusting the light in Lune's hand.

"Presto!" Sky held the sliver for Trasnet to see and then cleaned the wound, covering it with a large bandage. She sterilized her tools and put everything away except the flashlight, notebook, and cell phone. "Trasnet, now you have a battle wound, just like Hoppy."

Trasnet bowed to Sky and Lune. *Thank you*, he gestured, *for saving my life*. He took the two amulets from around his neck and gave the amulet from his mother to Lune and his father's amulet to Sky.

"It's beautiful," Sky said, admiring the ancient, braided leather rope with a tiny stone flecked with gold tied in the center. "But I can't take this." She handed it back.

Lune pushed it back to Sky and wrapped hers around her wrist, motioning for Sky to do the same.

Sky understood and wrapped the amulet next to the watch—at least two hours to go at the rate its hands were moving. She looked out the windows—there were no bears or torches. In her notebook, she drew a mountain and a tree. Then, she clicked RECORD on her cell phone, pointed to the tree, and said, "Tree."

Lune and Trasnet signed and said, "*Conifer.* Tree." They were excited to learn Sky's Tall Tribe language.

Sky signed and said, "Tree. *Conifer.*"

Sky pointed to the mountain and said, "Mountain."

Lune and Trasnet signed and said, "*Berg.* Mountain."

Sky drew many trees and said, "Forest."

Lune and Trasnet signed and said, "*Silva.* Forest."

Lune asked to borrow the pencil. She drew a large tree with three stick people and a rabbit inside. She smiled and laughed as she signed and said, "*Conifer Magicae.*"

Sky laughed, nodded, and said, "*Conifer Magicae.* Magic Tree."

Within an hour, Sky had learned enough words and hand signals to learn about their tribe, the Tainted Ones, and that they were oppressed by a second tribe, the Powerful Ones, under a king named Loch.

"Why is Loch so evil, especially when the Moon is full? Is he a werewolf?"

"A what wolf?"

"A werewolf…."

"What's a werewolf?"

Sky's eyes opened wide and her face became very serious. "A werewolf is a human who turns into a wolf during the full Moon. If it hasn't learned to control its emotions, it goes around terrorizing humans and animals when the Moon is full. Then, *poof!* The next day it turns back into a human and has no clue what it has done—except for the blood stains under its nails and on its teeth."

Lune and Trasnet stared at Sky, eyes wide open.

Sky's face relaxed a little. "Anyway, why would Loch tie up Trasnet and leave him to die?"

Trasnet shrugged. "We don't know. Okeanos, Lune's father, says Loch does it as a threat—to keep us oppressed."

"Or maybe the Medicine Man is right…maybe Loch is sick," Lune added.

"Maybe both are right," Trasnet said.

"Why don't you just leave?" Sky asked.

"We can't," Lune said. "We are not allowed the power of fire or spears, and we could not survive long without them. Besides, we are guarded."

"But you have a spear and you did leave to rescue Trasnet."

Before Lune could answer, Trasnet asked, "Lune, how did you get out? And why do you have a spear?"

"I have a secret passageway—you're too big to get through it. I never want to lose you. I decided I would rather die fighting for your life and our freedom than live a life of death and persecution."

"How did you get a spear?" he asked again.

"I taught myself how to make and throw a spear. I must return now, or another will die." She gave Trasnet the food and spear she had packed and told him where to go. "Little River Cave also has a tiny, well-hidden entrance—it'll be tight, but you'll fit."

Sky pointed to Lune's spear. "I have something like that, but it's much smaller. It's called an arrow. I shoot it with a bow." She eyed a spot on the wall, plucked an imaginary bow, and drew the arrow until it was taut just before letting it loose on its target. "Zip! Just like that, my arrow flies through the air and hits its target—dead on." She jumped up and down, excited. "I always hit my target! I'll bring my bow tomorrow."

On seeing this, with knowing looks, Trasnet and Lune said:

"Our prophecy is not lore and lies.
The Tall Tribe girl is here, beneath our skies.
Sky came to free us with her flying spear,
And her control over animals—far and near.
She does hold the sun in the palm of her hand.
Yes, we're sure Sky will—"

"Uh-uh. No. Nada. Nope," Sky said, interrupting them. "Many people, boys and girls, short and tall, have flashlights. Every Christmas, I get a new one in my stocking. And I get a new pair of scissors every year for my school box. I'm in sixth grade after all—or used to be until my parents ruined my life." Sky looked down for a moment, missing her school and her friends. "I have extras at home. Who wants the flashlight and scissors?"

"I can't take them," Lune said. "There would be another Killing Ceremony if Loch found them on me."

Sky gave them to Trasnet and showed him how they worked.

"No one has these things. No one, except you," Trasnet said, putting them in his cloak's pocket.

"Well, does anyone have a car around here? We can drive to a store in the nearest town and I'll show you all these things. And maybe we can stop at the police station and have them put Loch in jail."

"Yes, Sky will put Loch in jail!" Lune said with delight.

"No—no, I can't."

"Yes, I'm sure you will, but Trasnet and I must leave now."

Sky commanded the door to open.

Trasnet turned to Lune. "Please give Tunet a sign that I'm okay."

"I will." Lune made three hand signals while making five perfect sounds: the coo of a dove, the flap of a large bird's wings, and three hoots of an owl.

Sky thought she had never heard such perfect imitations. "What did that mean?"

"I can't tell you. It's the Tainted Ones' secret language," Trasnet said. "It's important for us to able to communicate in many ways. Sometimes, we need to inform others silently, through signing. Other times, we need to speak loudly in our secret language so the Tainted Ones can hear us no matter where they are in the kingdom." He turned to Lune. "Now, we have a fourth language—Sky's Tall Tribe language."

Before Sky could reply, Trasnet and Lune slipped out the door. Trasnet dodged deep into the woods while Lune slipped into the Icy Meadow.

Sky watched them vanish. Just before she commanded the door to close, she heard the loud coo of a dove, a great bird taking flight, and three hoots of the owl.

"Hoppy, everyone seems to know how to disappear." She chuckled as she checked the watch. The hand was nearly to *Time Expired*. "We should disappear within a half hour."

Exhausted, they lay on the floor, wishing they had a blanket.

Hoppy looked deep into Sky's eyes and said, "I think we should stop pretending to be mad at Mama and Papa. I like the farm."

"I'm not sure I like the farm yet, but I'll stop being mean to them if you promise to keep this a secret for a while. Otherwise, we'll never have any friends."

Sky stared at the ceiling, fighting sleep. She saw the faint outline of a square in the ceiling, about five feet by five feet. Inside the square outline, there was a tiny circle, no bigger than a quarter. She got her binoculars out of her backpack and saw the word *Press* engraved in the tiny circle. Finally, she lost the battle with sleep.

Sky and Hoppy woke to two clicks of the potting shed door at the exact same time as the metal door slid into the wall, exposing the old, oak door. The stopwatch hand pointed to the fancy *Time Expired*.

9

43 DEGREES NORTH, 2 DEGREES EAST

SKY PEERED OUT THE window. "We're home! Everybody's probably sleeping." She took off the watch and tucked Hoppy into the side pocket of her backpack.

"*Door Unlock.*"

She bolted through the door, slamming it shut. As she ran through the snow, she yelled over her shoulder, "*Door Lock.*"

Quietly, she opened the front door and tiptoed up the front staircase to her room. She tucked Hoppy under the covers. "I'll be back. I'm going to the kitchen to get a snack." She leaned down and whispered in his ear, "I love you, Hoppy."

As she headed down the back staircase, she was met by voices coming from the kitchen. *I'm in trouble*, she thought as she ran down the steps.

"I'm sorry I'm late. I...I fell asleep." Sky crossed her fingers behind her back.

Grandpa Doc checked his watch. "You're not late. It's only been a half hour since you unpacked. Dinner isn't for another half hour."

"Really? A half hour since your magic trick? Umm...hmm...Grandpa Doc, this house is really cool."

"Yes, it's beautiful and unique. My parents, Rio and Stella, built it before I was born."

"What about the barn and the other buildings?"

"They built them, too."

"Is there a stream running through the yard?"

"Yes, there is." Grandpa Doc's eyes twinkled. "Did you take a walk?"

"Uhh...no." Sky crossed her fingers behind her back again.

"The stream meanders through the property and flows down to the lake."

"Oh," Sky said, rubbing her forehead.

"That's a beautiful bracelet," Mama said, touching the leather wrapped around Sky's wrist.

"Oh, this...umm...Daisy and I made friendship bracelets for each other. Papa, what would you do if the king—I mean, the mayor of the city—was evil and tied people up and put them in the city park at night, hoping that a bear would come down from the mountain and eat them?"

Concerned, Papa answered, "I would do everything I could to help the people and bring their mayor to justice. Is that happening to someone you know?"

"No...umm...I was just reading *The Three Bears* and other books, thinking about the city, wondering what you would do, given you're a police officer and all. I think I would do the same."

LATER THAT NIGHT, SKY stood on her bed in her red-striped pajamas as Mama asked, "Where's the Arctic Circle?"

Sky traced a circle on her world map.

"Excellent," Papa said. "Now, where's Argentina?"

Sky pointed to Argentina. "Papa, what are coordinates?"

"Math, Earth, or celestial coordinates?"

"Earth."

Papa furrowed his brows as he walked over to the old chalkboard. "Let me think about how to explain this." He picked up a piece of chalk. The chalk squeaked as he drew a circle. "Imagine this circle is the Earth. Humans defined two important imaginary lines."

The chalk squeaked again as he drew one line across the circle. "One is the Equator."

The chalk screeched yet again as he drew a line down the circle. "The other is the Prime Meridian. Coordinates measure the distance from those two imaginary lines."

"Sky, can you show me the Equator on your map?" Mama asked.

Sky traced her finger over the Equator.

"Very good. The Equator is 0 degrees latitude. Can you show me the North Pole and the South Pole?"

Sky pointed to the North Pole and then the South Pole.

"The North Pole is at 90 degrees north, and the South Pole is at 90 degrees south. Latitude lines are imaginary lines that circle the Earth from east to west and run parallel to the Equator. So, if the Equator is at 0 degrees and the North Pole is at 90 degrees north, where do you think 45 degrees north would be?"

"Hmm, I think 45 degrees north would be about here," Sky said, pointing to the map and tracing an imaginary line that ran halfway between the Equator and the North Pole.

Papa nodded. "Anything on that line would have 45 degrees north in its coordinate. There are lots of places along that line. To narrow it down to a specific point, you also need to know about the imaginary line called the Prime Meridian. The Prime Meridian runs from the North Pole to the South Pole. As Mama runs her finger along the Prime Meridian, tell me which oceans, seas, and continents it runs through."

Sky studied the wall map. "North Pole, Arctic Ocean, Atlantic Ocean, Europe, Mediterranean Sea, Africa, Atlantic Ocean, Antarctica, and South Pole. Papa, what degree is the Prime Meridian?"

"It's 0 degrees longitude."

"Would 2 degrees east be just a little east of the Prime Meridian?" Sky asked.

"That's right. It's bedtime now."

"Can you turn my quilt into a tent under the stars, please?"

"Absolutely."

Mama and Papa tucked Sky in. After saying prayers, they each kissed her forehead and whispered, "I love you, Sky." They placed the quilt loops on the crystal knobs, turning the bed into a tent.

When they left, Sky drew a little star on her map where 43 degrees north and 2 degrees east intersected.

"Hoppy, wake up. Lune and Trasnet live in the mountains of Southwest Europe, probably in France.

We're not going to Daisy Riverstone's house tomorrow. You know how much her mom gossips. Within a day, the whole city would know. Then, the government would come and confiscate our UFO. No, we won't tell anyone. And…I thought of a great trick to play on Trasnet."

She put her collection of discarded cell phones in her backpack.

"Sky, don't forget that you gave your scissors and flashlight to Trasnet."

"Thanks, Hoppy." She put a pair of scissors and a flashlight in her backpack.

Before long, Sky and Hoppy fell asleep under the colorful tent as the moonbeams bounced off the snow and through the yellow-checkered window, casting shadows on the little bunny and the girl.

10

BACK IN THE POTTING SHED

AFTER TARGET PRACTICE ON Sunday afternoon, Sky took her bow and snuck out the front door.

"*Door Unlock*," she said, turning the fancy knob of the old, oak door. "No sign of the dragon this time."

Hoppy shrugged. "He's probably lurking under the huge lake that Grandpa Doc told us about."

Sky closed the door, opened her cell phone, touched RECORD, and dialed zero on the antique phone.

The metal door behind her slid quietly from the wall, locking her in.

"I'd like to call Lune."

"This is operator five-one-zero-three-seven. I'm placing the second call to Lune at destination coordinates 43 degrees north, 2 degrees east. Please hold while I confirm a connection."

"*Bonjour, c'est l'opérateur quatre-deux-huit-six-zéro. Vous êtes connecté,*" the second operator said.

"You have thirty seconds to deposit five cents for a five-minute connection. The potting shed will return to the origin when time expires."

"How long was I at Lune's yesterday?"

"The log indicates yesterday's call was a five-minute call."

"Why did it seem like hours?"

"Minutes at the origin are hours at the destination. Therefore, you were at the destination for five hours. You have fifteen seconds remaining to make a deposit."

"Does Lune live in France?" Sky put a nickel in the jar labeled *Deposit*.

"It wasn't called France fifty thousand years ago, but, yes, Lune lives in the Pyrenees Mountains."

Sky's jaw dropped.

The operator warned, "At the destination, open and close the door using the commands *Open Door* and *Close Door*. At the origin, lock and unlock the door using the commands *Door Lock* and *Door Unlock*. When you're outside the potting shed, keep the door closed. Please take a watch from the watch box. Your five-minute call will end when the time expires."

"Hoppy, we're in the Ice Age. That means our UFO isn't a really a UFO. It's a time machine!" Sky threw the bunny into the air and caught him on his way down. She took a watch from the box, checked the time, and did her best hip-hop moves.

Hoppy sang, "We're in the Ice Age!"

"Whoop! Whoop!" Sky pressed her fists down and swung her straight arms from one side of her hip to the other.

"We're in the Ice Age!"

As the phone went dead, she pressed STOP on her cell phone. Then, she pressed Hoppy's nose against the window as she grabbed her bow. "Look, it's snowing even more than yesterday. Come on, let's go outside and look for Lune and Trasnet. We can have a snowball fight with them."

Sky and Hoppy walked around and around the time machine, not wanting to stray too far.

LUNE WAITED PATIENTLY IN a tree in Wild Bear Woods, waiting for the Tree That Was Never There to appear.

"There it is, the Magic Tree" Lune whispered to herself. "I'm going to hide inside and scare Sky."

As sleek as an animal on the hunt, she weaved in and out of the woodland trees. Slowly, she approached the Tree That Was Never There and darted in. From inside, Lune looked up to West Shelf to make sure Loch wasn't there on his nightly walk.

SKY TIGHTENED HER PARKA hood to minimize the frigid sting on her face. "Where do you think they are, Hoppy?"

Hoppy shivered. "I don't know. I don't see anyone anywhere."

Sky scanned the woods one last time as she stepped through the door.

"*Close Door*," she said.

The metal door slid shut behind her.

"Boo!" Lune said, tapping Sky's shoulder.

Sky let out a bloodcurdling scream as she spun around and saw the White Doe staring at her. "Jiminy Cricket, you scared me. Why did you sneak up behind me like that? Take that mask off…please."

"Shh, you're lucky you closed the door. The Powerful Ones might've heard you."

Sky shook her head, annoyed with Lune for scaring her. "Don't ever do that again." As she caught her breath, she took her cell phone collection out of her backpack. "I have a trick for us to play on Trasnet." She smiled, pointing to the cell phones.

"Now, when I give you the sign, you say, 'Trasnet, I'm here...Trasnet, I'm here.'" Sky clicked RECORD and signed, *Speak.*

"Trasnet, *ana huna.* Trasnet, I'm here," Lune said, giggling after Sky clicked STOP. She was proud of herself for speaking in both her native language and Sky's Tall Tribe language.

They recorded Lune's voice on two more cell phones, leaving a three-minute delay on one. Then they huddled up with Hoppy and plotted their plan to trick Trasnet.

Sky handed two phones to Lune. "Come on, this will be fun. Let's go find Trasnet." She tucked Hoppy into the backpack's side pocket and grabbed her bow and quiver.

"Don't forget to close the door. You don't want to come home to a bear inside or worse—Loch." Lune pulled her mask over her face. "Follow me."

Lune raced through the woods and then realized Sky wasn't following her. When she turned to see what was wrong, a snowball hit her right on her face mask.

Fifteen minutes later, the girls ducked into a small, hidden crevice and followed a narrow path. Just before it opened to a great underground cave, Lune signed, *Stay.*

Sky watched Lune backtrack before losing sight of her. She waited, holding back her laughter—which would totally ruin the trick. Then, she heard the voice in the distance to her right.

"Trasnet, *ana huna.* Trasnet, I'm here."

"Lune?" Trasnet asked as he emerged from his hiding place.

"Trasnet, *ana huna.* Trasnet, I'm here."

Trasnet turned in the direction where Lune had left the second phone. "Lune? Where are you?"

"Trasnet, *ana huna.* Trasnet, I'm here."

Sky could tell that Lune was about ready to laugh, so she clicked PLAY. "Trasnet, *ana huna.* Trasnet, I'm here."

Confused, Trasnet turned and walked toward Sky, peering into the dark corner where she was hidden.

"Trasnet, *ana huna.* Trasnet, I'm here," Lune said, from her hiding place in the opposite wall.

Trasnet turned and drew his spear.

Sky clicked STOP and then PLAY at the exact same time as Lune said, "Trasnet, *ana huna*. Trasnet, I'm here."

The girls cracked up laughing and came out of their hiding places.

"How did you do that?" Trasnet asked, laughing. "That was freaking me out. I was beginning to think it was a spirit of the dark world or that I was going crazy from being alone."

"*Magicae*," Lune said. She gathered the hidden phones, showing him how they worked.

After laughing for a while, Trasnet asked, "Does Tunet know I'm okay?"

"Yes, Tunet knows, but the Powerful Ones don't. Loch is as crazy as always. Life will never change unless we do something. We need to plan the escape today."

Sky put the cell phone collection away, turned on her flashlight, and checked her watch. "For any good escape, the children need to be safe and sound first. Then, the grown-ups escape. But the escape never goes well and usually ends in a battle, at least that's how it happens in lots of movies."

Lune raised an eyebrow as she looked at Sky and thought about her comment. She turned to Trasnet and said, "Sky is right. The women and children are thin enough to escape through my secret passage tomorrow night after the Powerful Ones are asleep. You'll need to wait for me at the base of the mountain near the Ancient Tree and bring them to Little River Cave. But, if the snow stops, we'll have to take the long way, so no one sees our tracks."

"Is there really a river in this cave?" Sky asked, not meaning to change the subject.

"Yes, it's beautiful," Trasnet said. "But parts of the path are narrow switchbacks, and there are a few crevices we need to jump over. I'll take you there now." He turned to Hoppy. "Hoppy, are you tucked in? Are you ready?"

11

LITTLE RIVER CAVE

THE INITIAL DESCENT INTO Little River Cave was easy and fun. Trasnet, Lune, and Sky walked side by side on the wide path. Here and there, a stream of light from a hole above lit the way. Otherwise, they used the flashlights.

Trasnet stepped over a large rock. "So, we'll get the women and children out tomorrow night."

"Right, I'll bring them down to the base of the mountain by the Ancient Tree when I know everyone is sleeping," Lune said, jumping over a narrow crevice. "Sky, will you be here to help?"

"I sure will. Papa said that he would free the people from the evil king, and I will too."

THE PASSAGEWAY NARROWED, TAKING a deep descent. Trasnet led the way. "The men will be released from jail the night after next," he said, turning to look back at Lune. "Will they be able to escape through your secret passageway too?"

"No, that's a problem. They're too big for the narrow opening. Sky, do you have any ideas?" Lune looked over her shoulder at Sky.

"Hmm...can they just sneak out when everyone's sleeping?"

"That'd be a great idea except that someone is always standing guard at the entrance to our section of the cave," Lune said.

"Maybe try a distraction. Grandpa Doc told me distraction is an important tool in his magic bag. And when the men do escape, they must trick Loch. They must lead him in the wrong direction. Once they're sure they're not being followed, then—and only then—they backtrack to Wild Bear Woods and Little River Cave. But we need a backup plan in case the men are chased."

"You're right. The men must escape through Great Stag Forest, not Wild Bear Woods," Trasnet said as he stopped walking. He shined the flashlight on the pass in front of him. "Do you see? There's a two-foot-wide, twenty-foot-deep crevice right here. This is the only way. We must jump. I'll go first."

"Jump!"

"Jump!"

"Jump!"

"Now, just around this corner, the wall to our right ceases to exist for twenty steps. It gets a little scary—just go slowly," Trasnet said.

"Jiminy Cricket, you're not kidding—there's a huge cliff inside this mountain, like a miniature Grand Canyon. One slip on a rock and we're dead." Sky hugged the back of the passageway and didn't look down.

"If you look over the edge, you'll see Little River deep inside the mountain," Lune said. "That's where the Medicine Man and I find devil dust."

"I am not looking down," Sky hissed, edging her way along the pass.

"Careful," Trasnet warned. "This is where the path switches back and forth."

"Oh, great!" Sky held her breath as she hugged the wall.

"Three more steps and the wall will reappear. One…two…three. You made it."

"But there's nothing in front of you but a rock wall. How will we get to Little River?"

"I'm not taking you to the river. I'm taking you to the lake that sits above the river."

"Huh?"

Trasnet moved slightly, exposing a three-foot-high tunnel.

Sky shined her flashlight on the cave mouth.

"The lake is just on the other side. I'll go first," Trasnet said.

Finally, it was Sky's turn to crawl through the hole, and what she saw on the other side was nothing short of spectacular. Deep in the mountain, a beautiful underground river swelled into a lake. High above the lake was a beautiful ice sky made of stone that had to have been cut away millions of years ago and smoothed over the eons into soft, lofty curves covered with a thin sheet of ice. Sunlight entered the cave from a large hole above. It refracted in the clear water where it once again soared to the ice sky, only to be refracted again into the lake below. The sunlight was trapped—endlessly bouncing from the clear, fresh flowing water below to the icy ceiling that soared high above. The whole place was illuminated with a turquoise glow.

"Wow, this is awesome!" Sky sat on the lake's edge and checked her watch.

"Hoppy, you have to see this lake." She reached into her backpack's side pocket to help the little bunny onto her lap.

"Hoppy?" She looked in the other side pocket.

"HOPPY?" She began to panic as she unzipped the backpack to look inside.

"Hoppy, where are you?" She dug through the backpack.

Tears streamed down Sky's cheeks as she looked at both Trasnet and Lune. "We have to go." She frantically searched her backpack. "I have to find him."

12

HOPPY!

"HOPPY, I COULD'VE LOST you forever—you could've died. What on Earth are you doing down there?" Sky shined her flashlight into the narrow stone crevice that they had all jumped over on their way down to Little River. She brushed away her tears.

The little bunny closed his eyes in shame and whispered, "I don't know. When you said jump, I must've jumped too. I'm sorry."

"Oh, Hoppy, you don't have to be sorry. I'm not angry. You didn't do anything wrong. I was just scared. I thought I had lost you. I never want to lose you."

The little bunny—who had been so brave for the past hour in that dark hole—started to cry. "Are you going to put me on a shelf? I don't want to be safe and sound on a shelf. For decades, I stood in the dusty box, perched on the top shelf of Ye Olde Antique Shoppe, peering out my cellophane window, waiting to be freed and loved. No one ever played with me until the day you came in and rescued me. I never, ever want to be on a shelf again. I want to go on adventures with you, even if it means I might get hurt sometimes."

"Oh, Hoppy, don't cry. I'm not going to put you on a shelf. I'm going to get you out of there, and we're coming back tomorrow to help with the great escape."

"Sky?"

"Yes, Hoppy?"

"What time is it? I don't want our time machine to leave without you." Hoppy started to cry. "You can leave me here."

"Hoppy, I would never leave you." She checked her watch—the hand pointed to the fancy two. "We have plenty of time."

"Sky?"

"Yes, Hoppy?"

"It's a really long way down here. How are you going to get me out?"

"With my bow." She pulled the finest arrow out of her quiver. "I'm tying fishing line to the arrow, and then Trasnet will pull you up."

"Does that mean I'm going to have another battle wound?"

"Well, Hoppy, I'm afraid the answer is yes." She opened her pocketknife to the tiny drill and signed to Trasnet, *Drill a hole in the arrow, near the feathers.*

The little bunny closed his eyes in fear and nodded.

Sky cut a long piece of fishing line and signed to Trasnet, *Loop it through the tiny hole and knot it at the end.* She looked deep into Hoppy's eyes. "Hoppy, you know that out of every battle…"

Hoppy finished her sentence. "More often than not, something wonderful happens that would have never happened otherwise." He looked up at her. "Is it going to hurt?"

"It might hurt a little. But you know my arrow that has the tiniest of arrowheads, right?" Sky handed her flashlight to Lune and motioned for her to shine it on Hoppy.

"Yes," the little bunny answered as he started to shiver from nerves or maybe of fear; he didn't know which.

"That's the arrow I'm using." Her eyes never left Hoppy's as she signed to Trasnet, *Hand me the arrow and tie the other end of the fishing line to your wrist.*

"Am I going to lose my good ear to this battle?" Hoppy asked.

"Absolutely not, I'm going to pierce the tiny red patch in your beautiful quilted ear. And you know how good of a shot I am, right?"

"Yes."

Sky held the bow low to the ground so that Hoppy couldn't see it. "And you know that ear has very little pain because it's your battle ear, right?"

"Yes," the little bunny said, laying on a pile of rubble at the bottom of the hole.

"Let's practice once. I'll say *close your eyes, hold your breath, and count to ten.* And while your eyes are closed, imagine all the adventures we'll go on when you're out of the hole. Now, we'll practice once, and then we'll do it for real, okay?"

"Okay," Hoppy whimpered as he stared into Sky's eyes.

"Close your eyes." Sky peered down the hole to make sure Hoppy had closed his eyes.

"Nock—" She fitted the arrow to the bowstring.

"Hold your breath." She aimed at the tiny, red patch in Hoppy's quilted ear.

"Draw—" She drew the arrow back until it was taut.

"Count to ten." She heard him count.

"Loose—" The arrow pierced its target.

"You can open your eyes now, Hoppy. It's all over. Hold on tight and don't wiggle—Trasnet's bringing you up."

Hoppy was so happy that he started to cry.

Sky carefully removed the arrow and cut the fishing line. Then, she put a neon Band-Aid on Hoppy's ear and squeezed him tight.

"I love you, Sky," he whispered into her ear, pressing his face against her cheek.

She rubbed her nose against his and looked deep into his threadbare eyes. "I love you, too, silly rabbit."

Lune said to Trasnet, "She is most definitely the Prophecy Girl. Did you see that flying spear? She's going to free us!" She handed the flashlight to Sky.

Sky turned to Trasnet and Lune. "If I remember, it's you who came up with our great escape plan." She checked her watch and said, "Come on, let's go!" She tucked Hoppy in her backpack pocket and took off running for the cave exit. "We have one hour to get back to the time machine."

Fifteen minutes later, Trasnet signed, *Shh. We must slow down and put the flashlights away. We must be careful entering Wild Bear Woods. Trust me, Sky. We're just minutes away. Just give me a second to squeeze out and look around.*

Sky looked at her watch and signed, *Are you sure we're only minutes away?*

Trasnet nodded his head and shimmied his way out. A minute later, he gestured, *All clear.*

Lune, who had been going in and out of this cave since she was a small girl, slipped out easily.

When it was Sky's turn, she turned sideways, sticking her bow out first and then her body. She gave a great tug at her backpack, pulling it through. She exited the cave and entered Wild Bear Woods. "Geez, it's really snowing hard now!"

Quickly, they crossed the woods. Once Sky was safe in the Tree That Was Never There, Trasnet escorted Lune to the edge of Wild Bear Woods. He watched her cross the Icy Meadow and lost sight of her when she reached the Ancient Tree.

13

THE FULL MOON

LOCH PACED BACK AND forth in front of the jailed men as the Moon rose over Great Stag Forest, his antlers swaying with every turn. He huffed and puffed. He was enraged that the huge block of ice that his serfs supplied daily had nearly melted.

The Full Moon caught Loch's eye and hissed, "Don't worry that your water supply is nearly exhausted. I think the Tainted Ones need to suffer a little more. Give them half their food and water ration today."

Loch nodded to the Full Moon and then screamed at the jailed men, "Two days down, one to go! I'm sure you know who runs this show. Because of you, I have no ice. And, as punishment, half rations must suffice."

From under his gray wolf mask, the Medicine Man growled, "ENOUGH!" He slammed his crystal-topped staff against the Great Stone Shelf. "Just let them out of jail, they'll get your ice." He stared down his enemy, never losing eye contact.

Furious, Loch spun around so fast that the heavy antlers nearly pulled his mask off. He heard the guards chuckle as he thrust his antlers at the old man and hissed, "I don't think I heard you right, but I'll let it go, just for tonight."

Abruptly, Loch turned to his guards. "I'm taking my nightly walk to West Shelf, to view my sway." He thrust his antlers at the jailed men. "Do not let any of them get away." And with that, he followed the moonlight down the southwest ledge to West Shelf—the stone shelf that overlooked Icy Meadow and Wild Bear Woods.

14

HANGING ON BY A THREAD

INSIDE HER TIME MACHINE, Sky put her bow in its case and her backpack on the dusty shelf. "Hoppy, we made it," she said, brushing the snow off her clothes and backpack. "That was close. Thank goodness we'll be home in fifteen minutes."

"Hoppy?" She reached into the empty pocket.

"Hoppy?" She looked in the other pockets.

"Hoppy, where are you?" She opened the backpack and dumped everything on the shelf.

She grabbed her bear spray and flashlight.

"*Open Door.*"

Sky darted out, frantically shining her flashlight all around Wild Bear Woods.

"*Close Door.*"

She trudged through the freshly fallen snow and yelled, "Hoppy, where are you?"

A few minutes later, she saw the neon Band-Aid, just above the snow. She scooped up the cold bunny, held him tight to warm him, and then panicked when she saw her watch. "Hoppy, I can't see the time machine. I have no idea where it is." She shined the flashlight all around. "The snow is falling so hard that my tracks are already covered."

Lost, she felt like throwing up and shined the flashlight on the stopwatch—it was almost to *Time Expired*.

"Hoppy, do you see the time machine?" She shined the flashlight from one tree to another.

"I'm scared, Sky. The evil king will tie us up and leave us for the bear if he finds us. And, for all I know, he probably loves rabbit stew."

"What? Tie me up? Eat you?" Sky shrieked as quietly as possible, shining the flashlight all about the woods as cold snow blew in her face. "Hoppy, I've turned around so much that I'm lost."

The little bunny began to cry. "It's all my fault again. I got jostled out of the pocket when we squeezed through the cave exit. Fortunately, there was a tiny thread. I'm sorry. I was literally hanging on by a thread for as long as possible...."

"Oh, Hoppy, don't cry, it's not your fault. It's all my fault for putting you back in the side pocket and for keeping a stupid secret from Mama and Papa." She tightened her hood. "Jiminy Cricket, I just realized Mama and Papa will never find us if we don't make it back."

She checked her watch and thought, *I have less than ten minutes to make it to the time machine. I may as well start running somewhere...anything is better than just standing here.* Instead, she started hyperventilating.

Reading Sky's mind, Hoppy said, "Sky, running won't help if we don't know where we're running to."

Sky's head nodded in a jerky up and down motion as nerves twitched all over her body. "You're right, Hoppy. There's no sense in running." She shined her flashlight around Wild Bear Woods.

LOCH WAS SURVEYING HIS western kingdom from West Shelf when he noticed a small ray of sunlight in the dark of the night.

The Full Moon jeered, "Look who's here, Loch." It cast a light across him—making the shadow of a mighty stag appear on the mountain's wall. "Only one person holds the sun in the palm of her hand—the Prophecy Girl."

Loch's left fist curled in and out.

"She's here to free your serfs," the Full Moon sneered.

Loch choked the stone-tipped spear in his right hand as his left hand continued to ball in and out.

HOPPY LOOKED AROUND WILD Bear Woods. "Open the door, maybe we'll see the dusty inside."

Wrapped up in the thought of never seeing her parents, Sky didn't hear him. "What?"

"Open the door, maybe we'll see the dusty inside."

"Hoppy, that's a great idea. *Open Door.*"

Sure enough, the metal door opened. She made a run for it.

Thud!

A woodland vine tripped her, wrapping about her foot. "Get off me," she hissed. Twisting and turning, she finally broke free.

But, once again, one tree became another—they all looked the same.

"Which way do I go?" Frantically, she looked around the woods. Barely able to see through her tears, she looked down at her watch and saw the little compass with a teeny hand pointing to the fancy *Potting Shed*. She looked in the direction the compass pointed and raced to the time machine.

Thump!

A root, covered in snow on the forest floor, caught Sky's foot and threw her flat on the ground.

Suddenly, voices in unison chanted, "You'll never get home. Your tree is not like us. It is not welcome in our woods. Without you, it can never come back." It was the Wild Bear Woods, threatening her and Hoppy.

Furious at the woods, Hoppy said, "Don't listen to them, Sky. They're just trees."

Sky slammed her fist into the woodland floor, wiped the tears, got to her feet, checked the compass, and started to run again. This time, she paid careful attention to the fallen timber and shrubs on the snowy forest floor.

Whack!

A tree branch caught her neck, throwing her back to the ground.

Crack!

A rock smashed into her head as she hit the ground, sending a crushing pain through her.

"Mama and Papa will never know that we died in this forest. They will never find our bodies." Sky looked up at the trees. She looked at her watch. The hand was nearly to *Time Expired*. "This is the end of me." Tears flooded her eyes and trailed into the dirt on her face, turning it to mud.

"We can't just give up. I see the time machine. It's right there. Come on, Sky, get up!" Hoppy said, rallying her.

Encouraged, Sky hissed to the woodland, "You're just a forest with shrubs and roots and branches." She rolled onto her stomach, got up on her knees, checked the compass, and looked through the snow-covered brush separating her from the time machine.

"Shh," Trasnet said, crouching next to her.

Startled, Sky shrieked (but as quietly as possible), "Jiminy Cricket, now you're sneaking up on me too? You scared the heck out of me."

"I want to help you." He took her flashlight and turned it off.

Within a few seconds, Sky and Hoppy were safe and sound in the time machine. From the window, they watched Trasnet slip deep into the Wild Bear Woods as quiet and sleek as a wild animal—the snow covered his tracks. She lost sight of him just as he reached the entrance to Little River Cave. "From now on, Hoppy, we're leaving a note for Mama and Papa, so they know how to unlock the door, and who to call."

She scribbled a note, sealed it in a baggie, and pierced it with a zip tie. She held the baggie up and eyed the zip tie. "There...that should be a big enough circle  to slip over the doorknob. We'll leave it next to the phone. Before we make a call, we need to hang it on the outside knob of the old, oak door."

Not a minute later, Sky heard two clicks of the doors as the fancy hand hit *Time Expired*. "We're home, Hoppy! I can't wait to see Stella's observatory tonight."

THE FULL MOON TAUNTED Loch, "Are you just going let her walk in here and free the Tainted Ones?"

Loch glared into Wild Bear Woods, looking for the light. But it was gone.

"You weren't imagining it," the Full Moon snapped. "I saw it too."

"ARGHH!" Loch hurled his fist into the air.

"If I were you, I'd bring her in with a little bait," the Full Moon cackled. "Bind Tunet and leave him for dead in Wild Bear Woods. Then, watch and wait from the Icy Meadow. If she is who we think she is, then she'll free him from the ropes that bind him. And then, at that moment, you capture the Tall Tribe freak."

From high above Wild Bear Woods, Loch raised his spear and screamed for all to hear, "Tonight, we bind Tunet and leave him for bait—luring the Prophecy Girl in and changing her fate!"

Immediately, the crushing, rhythmic beating of the Powerful Ones' spears against the Great Stone Shelf began. The sound of the Killing Ceremony echoed throughout Loch's kingdom, from the western edge of Wild Bear Woods to the eastern edge of Great Stag Forest.

15

THE KILLING CEREMONY

LUNE HEARD THE CRUSHING, rhythmic beating of the Killing Ceremony as she squeezed into the narrow crevice at the base of the mountain near the Ancient Tree. She ran through the cave system. With each step, the beating grew stronger. She heard the women whimpering and the children crying as they woke from their sleep to the deafening noise. When she stopped in her secret cave to store her forbidden tools, she heard Loch roar, "One, two, three, four…surely, there must be some more!"

She squeezed through the crevice and into her tiny sleeping chamber as Loch bellowed:

"One step, two step, three step, switch!
Now tie a knot, that he cannot unstitch.
One step, two step, three step, stop!
Now tie a tight knot, right at that spot."

Lune ran to the back of the Tainted Ones' line, scooped up a small child who was falling behind, and heard Loch yell:

"Five, six, seven, eight,
Not even one had better be late.
Women and children kneel over there.
Keep going…don't stop and stare."

As Lune stepped onto the Great Stone Shelf, she caught Tunet's eyes. When no one was watching, she signed, *I will rescue you.*

A moment later, Loch screamed in her ear, "Put that child down, he's not frail. And now, my dear, you'll stay in jail."

Lune put the child down and walked through the jail gate, into the depth of the prison.

Loch blared like a horn:

"Tonight, there'll be no huffing,
And certainly, no puffing.

No, tonight, I'll get straight to the point.
But I promise you, I will not disappoint.
The Prophecy Girl is somewhere out there.
I'll catch her and kill her—she doesn't have a prayer.
I'm luring her in, using Tunet as bait.
Before she knows it, the girl will meet her fate.
Okeanos, you'd better hope the Prophecy Girl is found.
Because next, your daughter, Lune, will be bound."

Lune sat next to her father at the back of the jail. Without anyone noticing, she signed to him, *We must save Tunet. Then, we all need to escape—women and children first.* From the corner of her eye, she studied the thin leather ropes that held the jail bars in place as Loch howled:

"Guards, make sure you have them all.
Count the Tainted Ones, mixed of Powerful and Tall.
One, two, three, four, five, six, seven...
There's another four, making the total eleven.
Constantly be counting, without going insane,
In there, be sure the eleven remain.
Three more days in the jail...just a little pain,
But we'll refill the water, so do not complain.
For three hours, tomorrow at ten,
I'll let two of you out once again.

Just for a little, under the heaviest of guard,
Two of you will fetch me ice in the yard.
A big block of ice for the Powerful Ones will do.
And one small block for the Tainted Ones too."

As the antlered monster returned to center stage, Lune cringed as she watched him heat the tip of the ancient ceremonial spear in each fire.

Slowly, Loch dragged the hot tip of the spear across Tunet's cheek and hissed, "If the lioness doesn't make the kill, then the buzzards most certainly will." He paused, staring at the bloody, burnt cut on Tunet's face.

Lune knew it was devil dust time and saw Loch's eyes bulge as he looked around for the Medicine Man before looking up to the Moon.

The Full Moon belittled Loch. "You're weak. You can't even control the Great Gray Wolf. What good are his medicinal powers to you if he's never around? Are you going to let the others see how powerless you really are?"

Loch screamed:

"No need for the hullabaloo of the devil dust.
It's just nonsensical stuff that no one can trust.
There's no need for the crazy man's black magic today.
Come on, everyone, let's get this march underway."

Lune's mind raced, *How do I escape?* But her thoughts were interrupted by Loch's blustering:

"We're off to the woods. I'll take the lead.
Come on, let's go, let us proceed.
Let's keep this orderly, they'll be no stampede.
Oh, Tainted Ones, your hopes of being freed,
All that will vanish today, that's guaranteed.
I concede that my greed
Will keep your breed from being freed.
And that, my friends, is guaranteed.
Now, off to the woods, to Tunet's death indeed.
Then back to the Icy Meadow we'll recede.
There, we'll wait for Prophecy Girl to intercede.
Then, I'll spear the Tall Tribe freak and watch her bleed.
Bleed to her death…hah! I will succeed!"

Just before they marched down the southwest ledge, Loch yelled to the jail guards, "I don't hear you counting—make sure the jailed don't escape. One, two, three, four, five, six, seven—add four more, that makes eleven."

The jail guards started counting, again and again, in the required rhyme:

"Okeanos, the Black Bear is one.
Lune, the White Doe, makes two.
Together, the Tainted men make nine.
One plus one plus nine is eleven, we're fine."

From a corner in the back of the jail, Lune watched Loch lead the march to Wild Bear Woods, wishing she had a pair of scissors.

16

STELLA'S OBSERVATORY

STELLA'S OBSERVATORY LOOKED LIKE a fancy, oversized silo. Like the potting shed, the massive cylindrical structure was made of tightly stacked, finely cut, heavy stone and had a huge, oak door that was reinforced with ancient, hand-forged, iron braces. Windows spiraled upward toward the domed metal roof.

Sky lagged behind Mama, Papa, and Grandpa Doc. "Hoppy, keep your eyes open for that sneaky dragon," she whispered as they stepped onto a narrow wooden bridge and crossed the frozen stream.

Just as they reached the foreboding door, Sky found another long, pointed stick on the snow-covered ground.

In her best King's English, she held her sword high and interrogated the castle, "Yu' must be the neighborin' kingdom. I see yu' have a fancy drawbridge to cross yur moat!"

She looked back at the moat and readied her sword.

Crack!

The ice shattered, like glass.

Snap!

A split-tailed dragon sprang onto the drawbridge and growled under its fiery breath.

Sky held her sword high and then lunged at the dragon. She stared deep into its eyes. "What's the magic word to open yur fancy door? Abracadabra? Open sesame? Or maybe...*Door Unlock?*" Before she finished her interrogation, the dragon was gone.

Hoppy shivered as he whispered from the side pocket of the backpack, "I thought we were keeping the magic word a secret?" He nodded his head toward Mama, Papa, and Grandpa Doc.

Sky noticed everyone looking at her and faked a laugh. "It's a pretty fancy-looking building. Looks like a castle, don't you think?" By the time she looked up at the sword, it had turned back into an ordinary stick, so she dropped it to the ground.

Grandpa Doc's eyebrows were still raised high as he winked at Sky and said, "No magic word for this door, just a key. Welcome to Dr. Stella's observatory. She was an astrophysicist."

"An astro what?" Sky asked.

"Astrophysicist. An astrophysicist applies the laws of physics and chemistry to explain the birth, life, and death of stars, planets, galaxies, nebulae, and other objects in the universe." With a wave of a hand, Grandpa Doc lit the interior.

A wide, wooden, spiral walkway circled up and around the interior stone core. "Stella loved the Rundetårn—the round tower—in Denmark. It's the oldest functioning observatory in Europe and the inspiration for her workshop."

"Mama and Papa, do you want to race to the top? Ready, set, go. See you at the top, Grandpa Doc."

At the top, the spiral walkway leveled into a great circular room under a domed roof. The room housed an enormous telescope, an oak ladder with several large viewing platforms, a massive desk, and a machine attached to a rail on the wall. The telescope, desk, and machine were each encased in a glass box.

Sky ran around the room as she waited for Grandpa Doc. "Isn't this amazing, Hoppy?" She pressed his nose against the desk's glass box. "Look at the cool globes—there's the Earth…and the Moon…and Saturn…." Then, she saw a massive, leather-bound, drawing book and drawing tools: protractors, rulers, pencils, and pens. "I wonder what's in Dr. Stella's notebook. Do you think Grandpa Doc will let me have a desk up here?"

"Absolutely! I can't think of anything Stella would want more than her great-granddaughter's desk next to hers."

Sky did a little twirl as she threw Hoppy in the air and caught him on his way down. "Oh, Grandpa Doc, I love it here!"

"Me too."

"But, why is everything in a glass box?"

"To keep the dust off, of course." He pressed a button on the wall, and the lids of the three boxes opened gracefully. The glass boxes slid into the floor and out of view.

"Wow!"

"Pretty amazing, huh? You'll see Stella's technology is very advanced." Grandpa Doc took Sky's hand and walked over to Stella's desk. He carefully opened the leather-bound book, exposing the page tabs—hundreds and hundreds of tabs. A tab for the Moon, tabs for each sea and crater on the Moon, tabs upon tabs for each planet, tabs for galaxies, tabs for nebulas—tabs for everything. He opened the book to the tab labeled *Moon*, exposing Stella's magnificent drawing and her notes.

"My drawing of the Moon looks like Stella's." Sky got her notebook out of her backpack and placed it on the desk.

"They're remarkably similar," Grandpa Doc said, ruffling Sky's hair. "I think you're on your way to becoming an astrophysicist." He pointed to the number in the upper right corner of Stella's drawing. "We'll enter that number into the old, brass elevator control pad that's embedded in the desk. Stella always loved incorporating what she called ancient artifacts into her inventions. What's the number associated with this drawing?"

"Five-seven-three."

"Five-seven-three," Grandpa Doc repeated, pressing the numbers into the control pad.

"Just to confirm, you'd like to see the Moon, correct?" the elevator operator asked.

Hoppy's eyes opened wide. He whispered into Sky's ear, "I'm sure that's the same voice as the potting shed operator. Ask her a question so we can hear her voice again."

Sky looked at Hoppy and then at the keypad. "How far is it to the Moon?"

Grandpa Doc chuckled a little as he looked at Sky. "The voice is Stella's. I'm sure it's just some sort of recording she made. I doubt specific questions can be answered."

The elevator operator interrupted, "I can answer that question. The Moon's orbit is not a perfect circle, so it's not always the same. Tonight, it's 238,100 miles from Earth. Please press ENTER if you'd like to view the Moon."

Everyone's jaw dropped, except Sky's. She stuck her nose in the air and pranced around with Hoppy. "Kids are just more curious than adults. You've all lost your imagination. If you had some, you'd realize that we're in an ancient castle that was built by some advanced society that ruined their own planet, so they traveled here and entrusted Stella with all their knowledge and made her queen of this land and queen of that land…queen of all the land!"

Hoppy's eyes bored into Sky's as he whispered, "What are you doing? You just told them about the kingdom of the potting shed. You're telling them all our secrets."

Sky smiled sheepishly, realizing Hoppy was right. She'd divulged all their secrets. She changed the subject. "Can I press the button?" Without waiting for permission, she pressed ENTER, and the machine on the wall slid along the rail until it reached its destination.

Grandpa Doc looked up to the ceiling. "Look, a pulley in the machine is removing a roof panel to reveal the Moon. Now, watch the telescope and ladder move into place. Voilà! Come on, everyone, up to the viewing platform."

As soon as everyone had climbed the ladder, Grandpa Doc waved his hands and the lights went out. "Pure darkness…that's why Stella built her observatory here."

17

THE DEMON INSIDE

EXCEPT FOR THE MOONLIGHT, the sky was black as Loch led the procession of guards to Wild Bear Woods. There, he raised his spear high above his antlers and shouted:

"Drop Tunet here as bait.
Then we're off to Icy Meadow, where we'll wait.
When the Prophecy Girl is about to free Tunet,
I'll catch her and kill her. Then, we'll go on our way,
Leaving Tunet tied and bound for the lioness's prey."

Loch turned abruptly, following his guards out of the woods.

Tunet gnawed at the thick leather that gagged him and tried to rock to a standing position, but it was no use—his limbs were bound to his body.

FARAWAY, IN A DARK corner of the jail, Lune tried to untie the knots that held the jail bars in place, while Okeanos kept guard. But the knots were too tight.

The jail guard thought he heard a noise deep inside the prison walls. He turned in the direction of the sound but only saw Lune, the White Doe, sitting on a boulder. He watched her for a few minutes.

As soon as the guard stopped watching, Lune wrestled the jail bar's leather knots.

IN WILD BEAR WOODS, Loch turned and smirked as he watched Tunet struggle. "Tunet," he howled, "you'll never get off the ground. Your limbs and your body are too tightly bound."

Tunet continued to struggle, knowing he had to save himself because Lune was locked up in jail.

Loch hissed, "It's not you who I want. You are just bait. It's the one with the sun in her hand, the Prophecy Girl, who I want to terminate." Then, he turned and followed his guards.

Trasnet watched from his hiding place behind a dense tree. At the exact moment that he stepped out, Loch turned to heckle Tunet again. Trasnet became perfectly still, blending into the woods, watching Loch's every movement.

Loch raised his eyes to the Moon and then abruptly turned to follow his men out of Wild Bear Woods and into the Icy Meadow.

Quickly, Trasnet untied Tunet's gag and then used the scissors Sky had given him to cut the leather strips that bound Tunet's limbs to his body. Together, they slipped deep into the woods.

When Loch and his men arrived at the center of the Icy Meadow, they turned to watch and wait, but Tunet was not there!

Furious, Loch roared for all to hear, "She came and she went without any sound. She came and she went with no light around. She freed him within minutes, even though he was completely bound. If it takes me until my last breath, she will be found. And I will remain the ruler—gowned and crowned!" He thrust his antlers at his men and then snapped his head up. His left fist rolled in and out of a ball as his right fist choked his spear. He looked up to the Moon. "ARGHH!"

The Full Moon snapped, "Your men must be idiots. How could not even one of them hear the boy being freed? Give them a little push to help them home."

Loch turned to the first guard and shoved him in the chest. "You are all good for nothing. Did not even one of you hear a thing?" He pushed the guard in the chest again. "You're just a bunch of ding-a-lings. None of you are good enough for this king."

Loch didn't notice the pain in his guards' eyes, how he had hurt them, or their silent sighs.

As they climbed the southwest ledge, Loch lost all touch with the outside world, and everything became dark as he went inside his own head.

Because Loch saw nothing except his imagined thoughts, a small lip along the mountain ledge caught his toe—throwing him to the ground, ripping his skin, and tossing the heavy antlered crown from his head. Warm blood gushed from Loch's cheek, nose, and hands.

The Full Moon taunted, "Really, Loch? You're weak."

Loch pounded his fist into the rocky floor as he spat the blood from his mouth. He looked up at the Moon, struggling to get up.

Loose stones on the mountain ledge pulled Loch's foot out from under him, throwing him to the ground again.

"You let the Prophecy Girl get away," the Full Moon jeered. "You don't deserve to be gowned and crowned."

Loch slammed his bloody fist into the ground and stood up. He looked down at the Icy Meadow and Wild Bear Woods. Finally, he snapped his head to the Moon and shouted, "For as long as I stand, I will be king of this land!"

18

THE BEGINNING OF TIME

GRANDPA DOC TAPPED HIS wooden pointer against the long table in the sunroom.

Tap! Tap! Tap!

"Attention! I am the Monday teacher. Mondays will be dedicated to history in the morning and math in the afternoon," Grandpa Doc said. "Our history syllabus for the year includes a complete overview of the Earth since the beginning of her time—nearly five billion years ago. Once we complete the overview, we'll dig deep into specific time periods. For example, we might choose to explore the Mesozoic Era when dinosaurs ruled the Earth or the migration of humans over the great ice bridges."

"This is going to be fun," Hoppy whispered.

Tap! Tap! Tap!

"I expect your full attention," Grandpa Doc said. "The syllabus includes several field trips."

"Hooray, I can't wait. This is going to be the best class ever," Sky said.

TAP. TAP. TAP.

"Does anyone have any field trip suggestions?" Grandpa Doc asked.

Sky raised her hand high and waved it all around.

"Yes, Sky?"

"Let's go to the Ice Age!"

"Hmm...I'm not sure I remember seeing an Ice Age exhibit at the city's museum."

Sky raised her hand high and waved it frantically again.

"Yes, Sky?"

"We can go there in our time machine!"

Hoppy turned in his chair, looked directly at Sky, and whispered, "You just told him our secret."

"I mean...we can travel there in our imaginary time machine. We'll use our imagination and make a cave right here in our classroom and pretend that we have to melt ice by the fireplace to have any chance of having some water to drink."

"The idea of a time machine is very interesting. Anything is possible—one invention leads to another. I have a magic trick about invention...I think I can work it into today's lesson."

"Hooray! We love magic tricks," Sky and Hoppy shouted, dancing around the room.

"Get your coats and boots on. We're going on a field trip to the firepit—that's where the story begins."

"FOR HUNDREDS OF THOUSANDS of years, humans have gathered around fires to keep warm and safe...and to tell stories," Grandpa Doc said. He picked up a round stone from the ground and held it high. He placed it back on the ground and flicked it into a spinning motion. As it rotated on its axis, the enchanted stone became a tiny Earth, no bigger than a golf ball—spinning and spinning, around and around.

"Real or magic?"

Before they could answer, Grandpa Doc continued, "Lots of things may seem like magic, especially when the technology is not commonplace or doesn't even exist yet. Even for me, there are lots of things that exist now that couldn't have possibly existed when I was a child. For example, a cell phone never existed when I was a child because it needed other discoveries to precede it. Just because something doesn't exist now, doesn't mean that it will never exist or that it never existed." He paused, making sure they understood his point.

"Let's start with the first human invention—the stone." He picked up another small stone and playfully tossed it from one hand to another.

"Hundreds of thousands of years ago, one of our ancestors was either extremely frustrated by their inability to crack open a nut or was scared to death because some big animal was chasing them. Whatever the reason, they picked up a stone and used it. It became a tool—the first of many tools. With time, they discovered they could shape stones into different types of tools and even weapons."

Grandpa Doc held the stone high in the air and gave it a quick twist with his thumb—the stone became an arrowhead.

"Real or magic?"

Without giving them time to answer, he said, "The Stone Age lasted a very, very long time. It only ended about eleven thousand years ago when humans discovered metals, ushering in the Bronze Age. But let's not jump ahead of ourselves. Let's go back hundreds of thousands of years to the second great discovery of the Stone Age—the ability to control fire."

He flipped the arrowhead into the air. As it fell to the Earth, it turned into two stones. He caught the stones and struck one against the other, sending a spark through the air and onto the unlit campfire, where it caused the wood to ignite.

"And just like that, one little spark, one little idea turns into another little idea. That's how change happens. That's how things are invented."

The little spark became a flame.

"Real or magic?"

"That was real! Even we know how to start a fire," Sky and Hoppy shouted at the same time.

"Fire wasn't always easy to create," Grandpa Doc said. "The control of fire changed everything. For hundreds of thousands of years, our ancestors' tools were stones and fire. And that was it, for a very long time."

Grandpa Doc gave them a minute to consider that. "Let's continue our lesson on invention by fast-forwarding to about fifteen thousand years ago when humans began to domesticate animals." Grandpa Doc whistled for Hope, and the dog ran to his side.

"Real or magic?"

"Of course, pets are real," Sky said, petting Hope.

"Yes, but to someone living fifteen thousand years ago, that would've seemed like magic. Some might have even called it black magic because it would be very frightening to see a wolf walk alongside a human if you had never seen that before." For a few minutes, he enjoyed the warmth of the fire and watched Sky snuggle with Hope.

"A few thousand years later, humans learned to grow food. To us, domesticating animals and planting gardens is commonplace, but ten thousand years ago, those were big changes that freed up people's time, giving them time to invent wheels and boats...paper and ink...art and music. One invention led the way to another. Inventions came faster and faster...just think of what we have now: telephones, cars, planes, televisions, computers, and gadgets galore."

Grandpa Doc paused, looking at the fire, deep in thought. "I can't imagine the things that will exist ten thousand years from now. Even if I knew, you probably wouldn't believe me—you'd probably think it was magic."

Sky was so excited that the words ran out her mouth. "Ten thousand years from now, they have time machine UFOs. And when the time machine arrives at its destination, it pretends to be the things around it so that no one can see it, and only the person who knows the secret word can get in. That's why you only see the shadows of the UFOs on the Moon and never the UFO itself—it has secret metal technology that, like a chameleon, lets the UFO blend in with its surroundings!"

Hoppy looked from Sky to Grandpa Doc and back to Sky. He held his paw to his mouth. "Shh."

"That is a very interesting concept, Sky. We'll have to explore that idea in science and math class." Grandpa Doc rubbed his hand against his chin and looked out the side of his eyes. Playing along with Sky's comments, he smiled and leaned in. "Do you want to tell me the secret word to get into the time machine that's hidden inside the potting shed? I never could get that darn door to open when I was a kid. Whenever I complained about it, my father would say, *'Hijo, esa puerta no se ha abierto desde que no sé cuándo.* Son, that door hasn't opened since I don't know when.'"

Hoppy opened his eyes wide, stared at Sky, and whispered, "Tell him you were just pretending."

"Oh, Grandpa Doc, you're so silly. There's no magical invention inside that castle...just a golden-horned dragon!" Sky raised her claws and pretended to roar fire at Grandpa Doc. "The dragon says he'll spare yu' death by his fire in exchange for the secret to just one magic trick."

Grandpa Doc chuckled and played along, pulling seven coins out of his pocket. "Do you agree they look like real coins?"

"Yes, but I can't believe you're teaching me a magic trick!" Sky twirled around and threw Hoppy high in the air, catching him on his way down.

"When you toss the coin in the air, it remains a coin until gravity takes over. Gravity's force disintegrates the coin and ignites the magic dust on the inside, resulting in a tiny firework display with all the pops, booms, and sizzles. Here, try one."

Sky flipped the coin high in the air. Sure enough, as soon as it started to descend, the coin turned into a tiny firework display.

Pop! Pop! Sizzle!
Pop! Sizzle! Boom!
Boom! Boom! **BOOM!**

"Wow," Hoppy said. "You're a magician now, Sky."

"Can I have one, please? I want to make a little magic bag to keep in my backpack."

"Sure, here you go, six magic coins for the fire-breathing dragon."

"I don't need all your magic coins."

"I have a lot more. Stella, my mom, made me a whole jar of them when I was a boy. Plus, she gave me a roll of magic metal, a big bag of magic powder, and a special handheld machine that stamps the metal, fills it with powder, seals it with another piece of metal, and then stamps it shut while embossing it with a coin-like image."

"What's the magic metal and magic powder made of?"

"I have no clue. Whenever I asked, Stella would say, 'It's made of magic metal and magic powder.' She never told me the secrets to any of her magic tricks." He looked at the watch his mother had given him and then back at Sky and Hoppy. "Eventually, I stopped asking."

Grandpa Doc ruffled Sky's hair, Hoppy's battle ear, and Hope's furry neck.

"Come on…back to the classroom, everyone. The wind is picking up." He threw snow on the fire, putting it out.

GRANDPA DOC TURNED ON the overhead projector and pulled down a screen. "Here's a globe for each of you." He unrolled a long piece of paper and taped it to the wall. "This is a timeline of the Earth's history. It begins nearly five billion years ago."

19

THE TIME TRAVELER'S CODE

AFTER LUNCH, SKY GRABBED her bow and snuck out the front door when Grandpa Doc was taking a nap.

"*Door Unlock.*" She turned the fancy knob of the old door, stepped into the potting shed, and closed the door.

She opened her cell phone and touched RECORD.

She was ready to dial zero when Hoppy stopped her. "Sky, don't forget the note." He handed her the little note that was inside the baggie.

"Oh, thank you, Hoppy."

No sooner did she open the door when the winter wind whooshed by, stealing her note.

"Geez!" Sky chased the note across the field. "Give me my note," she yelled at the wind.

Finally, she caught up with the note and snatched it from the wind.

She raced back to the potting shed, hung the note on the doorknob, closed the door, and dialed zero.

The metal door slid quietly from the wall, locking her in.

"I'd like to call Lune."

"This is operator five-one-zero-three-seven. I'm placing the third call to Lune at destination coordinates 43 degrees north, 2 degrees east. Please hold while I confirm a connection."

"*Bonjour, c'est l'opérateur quatre-deux-huit-six-zéro. Vous êtes connecté,*" the second operator said.

"You have thirty seconds to deposit five cents for a five-minute connection," the first operator said. "The potting shed will return to the origin when the time expires."

"Are you Stella?" Hoppy blurted.

"I am the computerized voice of Stella. I answer questions and make decisions based on the information she stored in data tables and the code she wrote that reads the tables. You have fifteen seconds remaining to make a deposit."

"Was Stella an alien?" Sky asked, putting a nickel in the jar.

"No, Stella was Homosapien with a trace of Neanderthal. At the destination, open and close the door using the commands *Open Door* and *Close Door*. At the origin, lock and unlock the door using the commands *Door Lock* and *Door Unlock*. When you're outside the potting shed, keep the door closed. Please take a watch from the watch box. Your five-minute call will end when the time expires."

"Hoppy, if Stella wasn't an alien, how did she invent all this?" Sky took a watch from the box and checked the time. As the phone went dead, she checked out the windows to be sure the coast was clear before opening the door.

Hoppy's face scrunched up as he thought about Sky's question: *How did Stella invent all this?*

"Jiminy Cricket, do you see what I see?"

"We're not in Wild Bear Woods." Hoppy shivered as he looked around at all the people who were clothed in the furs of wild animals. "We must be on the Great Stone Shelf."

"Oh, no, there's Lune. She's in jail!"

LUNE KNEW WHICH ONE was the Magic Tree, despite it blending perfectly with the treetops of Great Stag Forest. As she spied The Tree That Was Never There from her position at the back of the jail, she signed to Sky, *Don't come out.*

SKY AND HOPPY STARED out the window at Lune, the White Doe, and then turned their gaze to the other cloaked figures.

"Hoppy, the man wearing the stag head with the big antlers must be Loch."

Hoppy shivered. "He does look like an evil monster. Look at him pacing back and forth. If he catches us…I can't imagine what he'd do."

"He'd probably tie me up and leave me for the bear and eat you as rabbit stew."

"What?" Hoppy jumped into Sky's arms.

"I'm just kidding." She rubbed her nose against the little bunny's for a moment and hugged him tight. Then, a shadow caught her eye. "Wow! Look at that, Hoppy." Sky walked to the window on the back wall. "That must be Great Stag Forest."

"The time machine is suspended in the treetops," Hoppy said. "The trees are massive. And, look, it's not snowing."

"Thank goodness! Oh, look, there's the northeast ledge. That's how they get from the Great Stone Shelf to Great Stag Forest."

For a few minutes, they stood in awe of the magnificent forest. Then, they turned their attention to the Great Stone Shelf.

Sky peered out the window. "The man dressed in the fur of a black bear must be Lune's father, Okeanos. All the others in jail are dressed in the furs of brown deer, like Trasnet. They must be the Tainted men. I wonder which one is Tunet," she said, not knowing her flashlight had sparked a Killing Ceremony the night before.

Hoppy pressed his nose to the window. "Look, there's the Great Gray Wolf. Lune said he's called the Medicine Man."

"Look at all those pigs. Their clothes look weird, don't they? They're the same men who left Trasnet in Wild Bear Woods."

"They're wild boars, Sky, not pigs. Oh, no, Loch is coming toward us." Hoppy hid his face.

"Silly rabbit, he can't see or hear us. Don't be scared." Sky snuggled the bunny for a minute. "Hoppy, we have to help Lune get out of there. She was supposed to be leading the women and children in their great escape tonight."

For over four hours, Sky and Hoppy thought and thought.

The stopwatch was nearly to *Time Expired* when Sky said, "Our time machine will leave soon, Hoppy. We can't just leave her there."

"I have an idea," Hoppy said. "Do you see the sinews holding the jail logs together?"

"Yes."

"They're the same thin, leather strips they used to tie up Trasnet. Let's give Lune a pair of scissors."

"That's a great idea, Hoppy."

20

THE GREAT STONE SHELF

WITHOUT ANY NOISE, THE coin flipped over and over, high above the Sacred Stone Water Basin and beyond the roaring fires. When the coin could no longer defy gravity, it exploded into a tiny but loud firework display. It startled everyone.

While everyone was distracted, Lune quickly and quietly moved to the front of the jail.

Pop! Crackle! Sizzle!

Without anyone noticing, Sky passed a pair of scissors to Lune.

Sizzle! Pop! Snap!

Lune put them in her pocket and quietly backed away to her place at the back of the jail.

*Pop! Crackle! Boom! BOOM! **BOOM!***

"Who the heck do you think you are—tying up children and leaving them for the bears? Loch, *ana huna*. Loch, I'm here," Sky shouted.

Furious, Loch spun around. "None of you move, the Prophecy Girl's all mine. I'll catch her and bind her and leave her for the feline."

Sky responded in Loch's silly required rhyme and said very loudly to the Powerful Ones:

"Why do you listen to him? He's a bully, nothing more.
He's no leader—just king of his imaginary lore.
What have the Tainted Ones done to deserve this?
I'm sure he treats you no better—this isn't bliss.
Bullies are bullies, through and through.
How would you feel if he bullied you?"

Sky shined her flashlight in Loch's eyes, blinding him.

As she commanded the door to close, Loch hurled his spear and roared, "She doesn't deserve to be fed to the lion or the wild boar. I'll kill her right now and end the Tainted Ones' lore."

"Oh, no," Hoppy cried. "His spear is coming right at us."

Sky held Hoppy tight as she watched the spear and her watch. "Three, two, one—time expired!" She twirled, throwing Hoppy into the air and catching him on his way down. "Loch just tossed his spear over the side of the mountain into Great Stag Forest."

"He's probably furious," Hoppy whispered. "Is he going to take his anger out on Lune?"

"I doubt Loch knows we're Lune's best friends. Besides, I think he's so angry with me right now that he's not thinking about anyone else. I can just hear him bluster:

'Rack 'em and sack 'em, that's what I'll do.
Powerful Ones, all of you, except the jail guards two,
Hunt her down, then bring her to me.
I'll bind her and feed her to the fire diety.'"

"No," Hoppy cried. "I don't want us to be roasted over the fire."

"Silly rabbit, I was just making that up." She rubbed her nose against his and stared deep into his threadbare eyes. "I would never let anything happen to us."

FROM THE BACK PORCH, Grandpa Doc watched Sky and Hoppy giggling as they stepped out of the potting shed and into the snow. He checked his watch and said to himself, "Eight minutes—about the same as the other two times. Whatever's inside sure has made her happy." He scratched his head. "What did she say the magic word was?" He laughed to himself, went back inside, and prepared the sunroom for the afternoon class.

21

THE MEDICINE MAN

LOCH'S ANGER BOILED OVER as he watched his guards ascend the northeast ledge with only his spear in hand.

"You didn't find the Prophecy Girl or Tunet in all that space?" He snatched his spear from them and waved it over the entire forest. "She couldn't possibly disappear without a trace." He thrust his antlers at them and then held his head high again. "I order you all to sit upon the great boulders that hold the jail bars in place and count the prisoners again and again while I think and pace."

He looked at the Moon one more time before taking his nightly walk to West Shelf.

While he was gone, the guards took a break from all the counting and got some much-needed sleep.

An hour later, Loch returned to the cave after surveying his dominion. He was shocked when he saw his minions. "What are you doing? You're all asleep! You're supposed to be counting them, not counting sheep."

He paced back and forth, deep in thought.

Bam!

He ran smack dab into the Great Gray Wolf—the Medicine Man. Loch snarled, "Where have you been? Out and about in the ice?" He cocked his head from one side to the other. "You missed the Killing Ceremony, not just once, but twice. I think you've gone mad, maybe totally insane. I need a competent medicine man with good devil dust under my reign."

The Great Gray Wolf walked past Loch, toward the guards, forcing Loch to follow. When he was directly in front of the jail, the Medicine Man turned to Loch, nearly causing a crash, and chided:

"Oh yes, my cynical, mystical devil dust...
Which, when inhaled upon a great thrust,
Freezes the one who sniffed for ten minutes, not more.
And they totally forget what happened just before.
I looked and looked but could not find,
So off I went and found it stuck just behind

All my elixirs, mixtures, and potions of every kind.
Alas, I only have a little, only two handfuls remain...
For it is very rare and too difficult to explain."

Tired of having Loch in his face, the Medicine Man walked around him, forcing Loch to keep pace as he continued to confront him:

"But I have the devil dust now, you see.
And all this counting is really annoying me.
Plus, I'm sick and tired of all the required rhyme.
Can't you give it a break for just a little time?
I'm really getting very tired, please stop this show.
Just what I wanted...I've lured you all into a row.
Brown deer back there, please join us up here.
That's great...now, you're all perfectly near."

Frustrated with all the Great Gray Wolf's rambling babble, Loch could not resist pushing the squabble. "You're crazy...you're mad...and your devil dust is more than just a tad bad."

"Is it?" the Medicine Man said, smiling behind his wolf mask. Then, he threw a handful of devil dust right up all their noses. Instantly, everyone fell asleep—except Okeanos and Lune, who were at the back of the jail.

"For ten minutes, we'll finally have some peace."

The Medicine Man looked at Okeanos and Lune and said, "Come here."

He pointed his crystal-topped staff at the sorting guard. "Just look at the disgust on this wild boar's face." He pointed to all the other guards. "You can see they're all clearly tired of this place. One day, there will be the jolt of all jolts. And Loch will be in for a huge revolt."

For a minute more, the Medicine Man enjoyed the silence. He breathed in and out, thoroughly enjoying the quiet. "You did a nice job, cutting the leather and loosening a jail bar. You'll have to tell me about your new friend and her magical tool when all this is over. I'll slide in for a second to bring you some food and ice. When I leave, make sure you tie that jail bar back in. They'll all be awake soon…devil dust doesn't last long." The Great Gray Wolf walked into the jail for a few minutes, not more.

Five minutes later, the Black Bear and White Doe tied the jail bar in place just before everyone woke.

The Great Gray Wolf held its head high as Loch yelled:

"I don't hear anyone counting!
One, two, three, four, five, six, seven…
Add four more, that makes eleven.
The Black Bear and his little White Doe…
Add nine brown deer, that's how you know.
That crazy, old Medicine Man, there he goes.
Wandering off to who knows where, no one knows."

22

MATH CLASS

GRANDPA DOC TAPPED HIS wooden pointer against the long table in the sunroom.

Tap! Tap! Tap!

"Attention!"

"Good afternoon, students. Welcome to our Monday afternoon math class. Our syllabus for the year includes a complete review of basic math including, but not limited to, addition, subtraction, multiplication, division, order of operations, decimals, fractions, complex fractions, ratios, areas, volumes, and linear equations."

Sky slumped in her chair. "It doesn't sound like as much fun as history class."

"Math is super fun. With math, you can unlock many secrets of the universe."

"Really?" Hoppy leaned forward in his chair.

"How do you think Stella built such a magnificent observatory?"

Sky sat up on the edge of her chair and turned to Hoppy. "I think math is going to be really fun."

"Let's start with a game to see how quick you are at addition. That's where it all starts." Grandpa Doc smiled at his students and set a timer.

An hour later, the sunroom door squeaked open. "Sorry to interrupt class. Mama and I just got back from ordering baby chicks at the local farm store. They'll be here next week," Papa said.

"Hooray for baby chicks!" Sky shouted.

"I can't wait!" Hoppy said.

"We're going to town to get garden supplies. We're taking Hope. Do you need anything?"

"We're all set."

"Don't wait on us for dinner."

AFTER SCHOOL, SKY GRABBED her bow case. She double-checked the backpack's side pockets—Hoppy was in one and her arrows were in the other.

As she opened the farmhouse's front door, an icy wind raced by.

"Geez," she said quietly, pulling her parka hood drawstrings tight.

As she ran down the country lane, she whispered, "It's time for the Tainted One's great escape, Hoppy."

After she cut through the gap in the evergreen tree row, a winter wind smacked her in the face and tugged at her bow case.

Sky's eyes teared from the bitter cold. She hugged the case to her chest and pressed on toward the potting shed.

The wind swirled around, chasing her.

"*Door Unlock.*" She turned the fancy knob of the old, oak door.

As soon as the door unlatched, the wind forced it open, throwing her onto the dusty floor.

"Geez!" Sky stood up, planted her feet, and, with all her might, shut the door.

GRANDPA DOC STOOD ON the back porch, sipping his hot tea in the cold, blustery afternoon sun. He pulled his scarf tight around his neck, watching Sky escape into the shed. He checked his watch.

23

THE GREAT ESCAPE

"DON'T CALL YET, SKY. You were going to add to the note. You were going to write: *Ask for a ten-minute call—minutes are hours at the destination.*"

"Thanks, Hoppy." She scribbled on the note, placed it back in the baggie, and opened the old, oak door.

A gust of wind blew it wide open again and snatched the little note out of her hand.

"Geez!"

The mighty wind tossed the oak door back and forth as Sky scrambled to chase the note that swirled around the room.

"I got you now." Sky grabbed the note and the door at once.

The wind calmed down long enough for her to slip the note on the knob. Then, it howled again, making it nearly impossible for her to close it.

Once secure, she shook her head and dialed zero on the antique phone.

The metal door slid quietly from the wall, locking her in.

"I'd like to call Lune."

"This is operator five-one-zero-three-seven. I'm placing the fourth call to Lune at destination coordinates 43 degrees north, 2 degrees east. Please hold while I confirm a connection."

"*Bonjour, c'est l'opérateur quatre-deux-huit-six-zéro. Vous êtes connecté,*" the second operator said.

"You have thirty seconds to deposit five cents for a five-minute connection. The potting shed will return to the origin when the time expires."

"Can we make a ten-minute call?" Sky put a nickel in the jar labeled *Deposit.*

"Yes, the watch hasn't been set yet. I have edited the time to ten minutes."

Hoppy blurted, "What year was Stella born?"

"Stella was born in the year 6266. You have twenty seconds remaining to make a deposit," the operator replied.

"I knew it," Hoppy exclaimed. "If Stella wasn't an alien, she had to be from the future. In our history lesson this morning, Grandpa Doc taught us that one invention leads to another. Stella had thousands and thousands of years of inventions and ideas right at her fingertips."

The operator interrupted, "At the destination, open and close the door using the commands *Open Door* and *Close Door*. At the origin, lock and unlock the door using the commands *Door Lock* and *Door Unlock*. When you're outside the potting shed, keep the door closed. Please take a watch from the watch box. Your ten-minute call will end when the time expires."

Sky took a watch from the box and checked the time. Sure enough, the watch hand pointed to the ten and was barely moving. As the phone went dead, she checked out the windows to make sure the coast was clear.

"Jiminy Cricket, do you see what I see? This must be Lune's secret cave. I see her workshop where she builds the spears here and her herbs and meat drying over there, but I don't see her anywhere."

Hoppy shivered.

"Why are you shivering?" She hugged the little bunny tight.

"It just reminds me of the cave where I fell in that deep, dark hole." He shivered again. "I don't ever want to fall into any hole again."

"Oh, Hoppy, I don't blame you. I have an idea." She took the magic coins out of her pocket. "I'll tuck one of these in your pocket. If you ever fall into a hole again, just toss it high in the air when you hear me calling your name. Okay?"

"Yes, Sky." He shivered one last time. "But, Sky, this is the great escape, and there should be complete and utter silence during any escape."

"Well, I agree with you on that. But, if you get lost, I don't care about complete and utter silence. I just want to rescue you. You hear me…you throw the coin high if you're lost." She tucked the coin into the blue-checkered pocket sewn to his furry belly.

"Sky?"

"Yes, Hoppy?"

"We should be completely silent, right?"

"Yes."

"Let's wait in our time machine for Lune. She tends to sneak up on us, and we always scream. We definitely can't scream tonight."

Hoppy thought for a minute. "Sky, I don't think the coin should be in my pocket."

"Why?" Sky scrunched her face.

"If you throw me in the air, which you always do, I'll catch on fire when the coin turns into a firework."

"You're right, Hoppy." She took the coin out of his blue-checkered pocket. "I have an idea. We'll ask Mama to buy you a tiny flashlight that fits into your pocket. You can shine that if you ever get lost."

A few minutes later, the Great Gray Wolf peeked in the windows.

"It's the Medicine Man," Hoppy said.

The Great Gray Wolf pushed the mask back and signed, *Shh.*

"It's not the Medicine Man—it's Lune." Sky commanded the door to open.

Lune stepped in and signed, *Don't talk until the door is closed.*

"*Close Door,*" Sky whispered.

"Why are you wearing the Medicine Man's clothes?"

"The Medicine Man sees Loch getting crazier every day. It's a long story, but he wanted to help. If it wasn't for you and the Medicine Man, there would be no hope of freedom anytime soon. The women and children are ready to go, but I think I should give you a quick tour of this cave system first. It's best if you know your way around before we go to Little River Cave. No talking once we open the door."

For the first time, Sky stepped into Lune's secret cave. *It feels magical in here,* she signed.

"Do you see that, Sky?" Hoppy whispered. "Our time machine is pretending to be part of the cave."

Yes, it is, Sky signed, studying the metal exterior. *That makes perfect sense. Time machines need to blend into their surroundings no matter where they land on the planet.*

SIX HOURS LATER, THE women and children were settled in Little River Cave with enough fish and water to last a thousand lifetimes.

"I promise we will return," Trasnet said to the women. "No matter what, do not go back to the old cave."

Nix—who excelled at making a crow's caw—followed them to the cave exit where she waited to guide the men. She signed, *Godspeed.*

Sky checked her watch—one hour until the time machine leaves. *Hoppy and I don't have time to go to Great Stag Forest with you.*

We'll take you to the edge of Wild Bear Woods, Lune signed. *If we don't see Loch on West Shelf, you can travel the short distance over the Icy Meadow to the Ancient Tree. Your compass will guide you.*

Sky nodded and smiled as she held up her bear spray and bow.

Tunet stepped forward and signed, *You saved our lives and gave us the courage to fight for our freedom—even if it means we end up with some battle wounds.* He touched the wound where Loch had sliced and burned his cheek.

We will see you again, Trasnet signed with conviction as he looked into Sky's eyes and then Hoppy's. *Thank you for everything.* He gave them a beautiful smile and wrapped his strong arms around them both, giving them a big hug.

Promise me that I'll see you again, Lune gestured.

Sky laughed as she signed, *Stop acting like I'll never see you again. The Medicine Man will use his devil dust to put the Powerful Ones to sleep, and the men will escape. Hoppy and I will be back tomorrow.*

Giggles replaced the solemn goodbyes.

Together, they walked swiftly and silently to the edge of Wild Bear Woods. They looked up to West Shelf, making sure no one was watching. Then, they parted.

24

THE WHITE DOE

SKY SHIVERED. "WILD BEAR Woods is super spooky without Lune, Trasnet, and Tunet." She checked her watch. "We have lots of time to get to the time machine." She held her bow in one hand and bear spray in the other.

"Hoppy, do you think Loch was born evil?" Sky whispered. "Or do you think something happened and he turned evil? He definitely might be a werewolf—he probably has blood stains under his fingernails."

Hoppy shivered. "Let's not talk about him right now."

BEFORE ENTERING THE ICY Meadow, Sky looked up to West Shelf one last time. She whispered, "I don't see Loch or anyone, do you?"

"No," Hoppy whispered.

"Do you think the Powerful Ones know they have a monster ruling them? Or do you think they pretend everything is fine?"

Hoppy shivered. "Please stop talking about him."

HALFWAY THROUGH THE ICY Meadow, a chill raced up Sky's spine. She looked down at the little bunny, who was shivering in her side pocket. As she looked back up, something caught her eye. Sky stopped, crouching beneath a snowbank.

"Why did you stop?" Hoppy whispered.

"I thought I saw a shadow by the Ancient Tree, but I don't see it now. It was probably just bare branches moving with the wind."

"There's no wind tonight," Hoppy whispered. "I hope it wasn't Loch's antlers…they look like branches."

"It was nothing…just my eyes playing tricks on me."

They continued to cross the meadow in silence.

Sky thought of Trasnet and Tunet. "He kills people without even touching them—having others tie them up, cutting their face slowly with the burning-hot tip of his spear, leaving them in the woods for the bear."

"Please stop, Sky."

"Maybe the devil possessed him."

NEAR THE ANCIENT TREE, Sky and Hoppy looked up at West Shelf one last time. "No one."

"I don't think we're alone," Hoppy whispered.

"There's nothing but silence." Sky looked a little longer before turning toward the tree.

BAM!

Horrified, she squealed, "Jiminy Cricket! What the heck?"

Nine heads were hanging in a tree—brown, eyeless, deer heads with branches pierced through the cut-out eye sockets. A splatter of blood tainted each.

She dashed for the Ancient Tree, dodging branches along the way. As she turned toward the Ancient Tree, she ran smack dab into a black bear head with no eyes. Her heart pounded.

"Jiminy Cricket, it's Lune's father's mask. Hoppy, I'm so freaked out I don't know which way to go."

"Check the compass."

Trembling, she checked it. "This way." She sprinted, dodging around trees and then *boom!* She was flat on the ground. "What the heck? What tripped me?" She checked Hoppy and looked at the compass before standing up. "Where's the bear spray?"

As she reached for the spray, she saw gray wolf boots beneath the robes of a white doe who was leaning against a tree. She scrambled to her feet. "Thank God, it's you. Oh, Medicine Man, help us!"

Sky looked at the man under the white doe mask and only saw the whites of his eyes and blood trickling down the front of the white, fur cloak. She let out a hair-raising scream and saw hoof-covered hands holding the Medicine Man up.

LUNE, TUNET, AND TRASNET heard Sky scream. Trasnet signed, *Go south and meet the men in Great Stag Forest. I'll go north to help Sky.*

THE DEAD MEDICINE MAN dropped in front of Sky as she tried to make a run for it. She let out another horrific scream and then saw the mighty stag standing in front of her.

"You killed the Medicine Man! Are you crazy? All the Tainted Ones want is their freedom. Just give them their freedom."

"Never!" Loch thrust his antlers at her, trapping her. "Never, ever!"

Sky blasted him with bear spray, but it had no impact.

He whacked the can away, knocking her to the ground.

Agonizing pain coursed through her body as she writhed on the ground next to the dead Medicine Man. As she heaved in air, she wrenched to the side to make sure Hoppy was still in her backpack.

Loch hissed, "This is what happens to traitors. They're not bound…through their neck, a spear will be found."

As Loch looked to the Moon, Sky started to shimmy away.

Whack!

She felt his hand on her ankle as he pulled her back between his short, powerful legs and flipped her from her stomach onto her back.

"My guards are all asleep. Only I am awake.
The Tainted men are gagged and bound, each to a stake.
I'll let my guards sleep, the sleep that they're due.
When the Tainted women wake, they'll be tied too."

Loch hovered over Sky. He wanted to show his dominance a little longer—to show her that, of the two, he was the stronger.

"Oh, by the way, on this traitor, I found
These gadgets and gizmos, they're most profound.
They came in quite useful for cutting off the masks.
I can see they'll be useful for plenty of sinister tasks.
They're much better than devil dust any old day.
Quite honestly, I didn't need that old man anyway."

Loch leaned over Sky, dangling the scissors just above her face.

"You're a stupid werewolf!" she screamed, shoving her foot between his legs.

He gasped, doubling over with tremendous pain.

She grabbed the scissors and shoved him down with her feet.

AS TRASNET RACED THROUGH the Icy Meadow, he heard nearly everything and thought, *She's inside now. If she doesn't make it to the Magic Tree, I'll meet her on the Great Stone Shelf.*

SKY RAN AS FAST as she could through the great cave system. "It's going to be really close, Hoppy. If we do make it, do we free the men or ourselves?"

"Time will tell," Hoppy said, his body trembling.

25

A DANCE WITH THE WINTRY WIND

GRANDPA DOC LEANED AGAINST the porch railing, sipping his hot tea, watching the potting shed. As the wintry wind howled, he tightened the drawstrings of his parka hood.

THE ICY WIND DANCED with the little note inside the baggie—daring it to escape and run free from the doorknob that held it hostage.

GRANDPA DOC WENT BACK inside and refilled his mug.

THE LITTLE NOTE FLIRTED with the wind. It was so enamored that it was beginning to forget its love for the little girl and her bunny. And it had completely forgotten the secrets it held—including the secret to unlock the old, oak door.

26

TIME IS TIME

SKY LOOKED AT HOPPY. "One hour should be long enough to cut Okeanos and the others free. Then, we'll go home." She picked up the antique phone and dialed.

"This is operator five-one-zero-three-seven. Who would you like to call and for how long?"

"I'd like to make a one-minute call to—"

Sky turned to Hoppy, covered her mouth, and whispered, "Hoppy, we don't want to call Lune. We're the only ones who know that Okeanos and the others are tied to stakes. If our time machine lands next to Lune, the men will never escape before Loch returns."

"Call Okeanos," Hoppy suggested. "He's the one we want to be near anyway."

"I'd like to make a one-minute call to Okeanos, Lune's father," Sky said to the operator.

The operator responded, "I'm sorry, that's not a valid request."

"Huh?" Sky and Hoppy's eyes opened wide as they stared at each other.

Sky covered her mouth and whispered close to Hoppy's ear, "The operator was never difficult before."

Hoppy whispered back, "Honestly, I don't think the operator is really a person. She pretty much says the same things over and over—like a machine."

Hoppy turned to the phone and asked, "Why isn't Okeanos a valid request?"

"You can't call anyone within three hundred years of a logged entry's lifespan. You called Lune. Therefore, she is a logged entry in the table. You can redial your last location. Would that work?"

"Yes, thank you."

"I'm placing the fifth call to destination coordinates 43 degrees north, 2 degrees east. The date and time are based on the most recent call. Please hold while I confirm a connection."

"*Bonjour, c'est l'opérateur quatre-deux-huit-six-zéro. Vous êtes connecté,*" the second operator said.

"You have thirty seconds to deposit five cents for a one-minute connection. The potting shed will return to the origin when time expires. At the destination, open and close the door using the commands *Open Door* and *Close Door*. At the origin, lock and unlock the door using the commands *Door Lock* and *Door Unlock*. When you're outside the potting shed, keep the door closed. Please take a watch from the watch box. Your one-minute call will end when the time expires."

Sky took a watch, and the phone went dead.

Sky and Hoppy pressed their noses against the window.

"Phew—we're back in Lune's secret cave," Hoppy said, wiping his brow.

"*Open Door.*"

As Sky raced through the cave system, she whispered over her shoulder, "*Close Door.*"

And then she saw it and stopped abruptly—the watch hand was racing to *Time Expired*.

"Jiminy Cricket, the stopwatch is at the twenty, and it's going really fast. Hoppy, it's almost to *Time Expired.* What do we do?"

"Let's go home and call again."

She ran like the wind to the time machine.

"We'll have time to come back before Loch recovers—that was a really good kick you gave him."

"Fifteen seconds—"

"Sky, we need to take Grandpa Doc with us this time and make a long call. He'll know how to help Okeanos and the Tainted Ones."

"*Open Door—*"

In the distance, Sky could see the dusty inside.

"Ten seconds—"

She sprinted as fast as she ever had. "What if Grandpa Doc doesn't believe us?"

Hoppy hesitated. "Good point...I know. We won't tell him. We'll lure him into the potting shed and pretend to make a call. He'll be forced to come with us."

"Hoppy, hold on tight, we have one second...there's the door." Sky pushed off hard from the cave's stone floor, propelling herself to the door.

27

GREAT STAG FOREST

LUNE AND TUNET REACHED the massive trees of Great Stag Forest well past midnight. It was pitch black—dark shadows of trees layered upon black, empty space. They headed north until they were just below the Great Stone Shelf. They smelled the scent of the Powerful Ones' campfire, wafting down the northeast ledge. There, they parted. Lune headed east while Tunet headed northeast until they were separated by six hundred feet, the distance of two football fields.

"Caw...caw." Lune made two perfect crow caws and thought, *Now, the Medicine Man should be using his last handful of devil dust on the jail guards. It's time for the men to escape.*

As still as two deer in two corners of the vast expanse, Lune and Tunet became one with the shadows of the forest.

OKEANOS HEARD LUNE'S CAW, but he was gagged and tied to a stake on the Great Stone Shelf. And the Medicine Man, with his devil dust, was not around—Loch had forced him to go on a walk two hours before.

28

POOF!

SKY AND HOPPY SAILED through the air, straight to the door leading to the dusty room.

Poof!

The dusty room was gone.

"Jiminy Cricket!" Sky wrenched her body in mid-flight to get her legs beneath her, bending her knees as she landed to minimize the impact against the cave's hard, stone floor.

"What the heck? Why didn't the operator tell us that a minute was sixty seconds?" Tears welled up in her eyes.

Hoppy tried to comfort her. "If we had asked, I'm sure she would've told us that a minute is sixty seconds, and seconds are seconds. We left a note. It won't be long until someone finds it and, when they do, they're going to call Lune. Right now, we need to free the men and find Lune."

29

THE LITTLE NOTE

GRANDPA DOC WENT BACK outside. He checked his watch—over ten minutes had passed. He put his tea down, pulled his parka hood up, and crunched his way through the ice-covered snow.

THE DOORKNOB HELD THE little note with all its might as it fought the powerful wind.

THE LITTLE NOTE ADMIRED the wintry wind's strength. It wanted to fly away with it—to go on wild adventures to faraway places. As the battle between the wind and the doorknob raged on, the little note slipped over and under the knob, trying to decide which love to choose—the little girl or the wind's promise of wild adventures.

THE WIND SWIRLED UP and over the ornate spire, forcing the note to choose.

THE LITTLE NOTE MADE its decision—it chose the mighty wind and its promise of wild adventures.

30

O' SWEET FREEDOM

TRASNET SPRINTED THROUGH THE Icy Meadow.

LOCH GRABBED HIS CROTCH, still wincing from the pain of the Prophecy Girl's kick. Out of the corner of his eye, he had seen her and that little bunny escape into a tiny crevice near the Ancient Tree.

"You think you're slick…I'll put your little bunny on a stick," he said, gasping for air. "I'll roast him over a fire, you'll see." He hobbled to the tiny crevice. "And hear you cry, 'Just let my bunny be!'"

He tried to squeeze into the narrow cave opening, but his chest was too thick, and his antlers too wide. "When the rabbit is thoroughly roasted…into the soup, he'll go." Loch took a deep breath. The pain was nearly gone. "Then, to the flames, it'll be your turn to say hello."

The pain was gone. Loch sprinted—leaping over the dead Medicine Man and spitting on the nine blood-splattered deer heads as he raced by. He shot up the southwest ledge.

TRASNET RACED UP THE southwest ledge, knowing Loch wasn't far behind.

SKY SIGNED TO THE men, *Shh. I'm here to help.* First, she untied all their gags. Then, she began cutting the leather ropes that bound Okeanos to the stake.

The men stared at her—and her cutting tool—in disbelief.

THE SORTING GUARD WOKE, thinking he had heard a noise. He poked his head out from under his fur blanket and cocked his ear in the direction of the noise.

TEN MINUTES LATER, FIVE men were free. The other five were still bound to the stakes.

THE SORTING GUARD—WHO was too groggy from all the counting—couldn't keep his eyes open. He fell back asleep.

SUDDENLY, SKY FELT A hand on her shoulder. She sprang to her feet and drew the scissors back, ready to strike.

"Jiminy—"

Trasnet gestured, *Shh. I'm here to help.*

Angry, Sky signed, *Why did you sneak up on me?* Her body shook, releasing the fear. *How did you know to come and help? Where's Lune and Tunet?*

I heard you scream. I heard Loch say the men were tied to stakes. Lune and Tunet are in Great Stag Forest by now. They did not hear your struggle with Loch.

Don't ever sneak up on me again.

Hurry, Loch is on his way. Trasnet took his scissors out of his pocket and began cutting the leather ropes, too.

THE SORTING GUARD WOKE again. He was sure he had heard something. He sat up, searching the dark bedroom for his uniform.

TWO MEN WERE STILL tied to the stakes when Sky heard Loch grow nearer. "I'll kill that weak freak," he grunted.

THE SORTING GUARD'S HEAD was heavy, like a bag of sand. He was so tired from being overworked that he fell back asleep on his thick pile of furs.

FINALLY, THE TAINTED MEN were free.

Trasnet gestured, *Follow me.*

They stopped for a minute on the northeast ledge—just below the Great Stone Shelf.

Trasnet signed, *Today, we will escape without violence and become free people. Okeanos and Sky will go with me. The rest of you go south and then head west across Wild Bear Woods. If Loch follows you, don't worry. Keep going and don't turn back. When you're deep in the woods, caw three times. Nix will echo your call. Follow her sound. You will find the women and children there. Go now, quietly.*

As they waited for the nine men to descend the mountain, Loch was just above them on the Great Stone Shelf—grunting and groaning, mumbling to himself.

Trasnet signed, *He's surveying his eastern kingdom—Great Stag Forest. He hasn't noticed the men have escaped. Quiet.*

LOCH HISSED TO HIMSELF, "I know the Prophecy Girl got away. What do you want from me? What do you want me to say?"

The Full Moon sneered, "If you had just shut up and gotten the job done, she would've been dead long ago. But, no, you always have to gawk and squawk and put on a huge show. Have you even noticed what happened yet? Do you see who's gone?"

Loch turned and roared, "Guards!"

SWIFTLY, SKY, TRASNET, AND Okeanos ran down the mountain ledge.

At the base of the mountain, Trasnet signed, *Godspeed.* He watched Sky and Okeanos head north before he slipped silently into a southern corner of Great Stag Forest.

LOCH HEARD A NOISE and boomed, "There they are, in my sway. Hurry now, they're getting away."

The groggy guards were nearly by Loch's side, still fumbling with their cloaks—adjusting their snouts and cinching the wild boar fur around their waists.

Loch bellowed, "See…there they all go." He pointed to the forest and thrust his antlers at them. "Did you not hear them? Did you not know? Each one of you must be an idiotic, pea-brained bozo."

"Stop," the Full Moon scolded. "There you go again, ranting and raving. Stop the chitter, stop the chatter, and get to the heart of the matter."

Loch led the charge down the side of the mountain as he roared, "Go get them, my Neanderthals! Don't kill just one…kill them all! Who needs them to get the ice when I have you who will do the job just as nice?"

The guards stopped and stared at each other. They muttered under their breath, "We have to get the ice now?"

"What are you waiting for? Come on, move it, you mighty boars!"

31

MAGIC TOOLS: DISTRACTION AND DECEPTION

LOCH AND HIS GUARDS stopped at the base of the mountain.

Loch cocked his antlers to one side as he looked all around Great Stag Forest. "I know I saw Okeanos, the Black Bear. He has to be somewhere near, but where?"

"Look," the sorting guard cried. "I see them escaping down there."

"They are tainted, half-breeds, nothing more," Loch said, thrusting his antlers. "Let's hunt them down, you mighty boars!"

LUNE WATCHED LOCH AND his men chase the Tainted men. From her hiding place on the eastern edge of the forest, she turned on her flashlight for a minute. *Click...click.*

LOCH STOPPED ABRUPTLY IN his tracks, causing his guards to slam into his back. He tilted his head side to side—casting the antler's shadow first narrow and then wide. He turned to the sorting guard and hissed, "The Prophecy Girl is here, and she wants a fight. I'll give her a good fright!" He traced the tip of his spear down the guard's neck and then turned toward the direction of Lune's flashlight. "Guts and gore...I'll give you blood galore!"

SILENCE AND DARKNESS FILLED the ghostly space that separated Loch from Lune. As Loch ran toward her, Lune stood silent and still.

TUNET WATCHED EVERY STEP from his position in the northeast corner of the forest. *Now,* he thought, flickering his flashlight on for a minute. *Click...click.*

ANGRY, LOCH TURNED TO the northeast, dodging in and out of the familiar trees with his men close behind. "You think you're fast, do you? Holding the sun in your hand will not get you through. Very soon, your little bunny will be rabbit stew."

TRASNET FLIPPED A COIN high in the air from his position in the southwest corner of Great Stag Forest. When the coin could no longer defy gravity, it burst into a tiny firework display in the deep dark of the night.

Pop! Crackle! Sizzle!
Crackle! Pop! Fizzle!
Boom! BOOM! **BOOM!**

LOCH AND HIS MEN were close to Tunet when they heard the familiar popping sound and spun around.

Loch lowered his antlers, thrusting them forward. Then, he snapped them back up. "The Prophecy Girl thinks she's cunning with her pop and boom display. I'll show her that this is a game that two can play. She'll find out the hard way. Charge, my mighty boars, lead the way."

They rushed in Trasnet's direction, holding their spears high.

As Loch charged, he threatened, "I'm tired of your lore and sick of your games. For you, first anguish and pain when your bunny goes up in flames."

SKY YELLED FROM THE eastern corner of the forest, "Loch, *ana huna*. Loch, I'm here."

LOCH AND HIS MEN stopped. Their frustration and emotions crowded out their animal instincts. They did not see, hear, or smell Trasnet, who was just steps away.

SKY SHOUTED FROM THE east once more, "Loch, *ana huna*. Loch, I'm here."

THE GREAT FOREST WAS spine-chillingly silent and devoid of color—just two shades of unwavering black: the sheer black of the deathly air through which they could run and the solid black of gigantic trees behind which they could hide.

Loch pitched his ear here and then his other ear there, causing the mighty antlers atop his head to flow in an odd circular fashion. His guards, who were just behind him, did the same—they cocked their heads here and then they cocked their heads there, causing the long snout and tusks protruding from their faces to also circle around in a very peculiar way.

Then, in the icy, wintry silence, a crow cawed three times from a great distance away—the distraction was complete.

Caw!

Lune thought, *The men are near Little River Cave. Now, it's time for us to make our escape.* She touched STOP on her cell phone.

Caw!

She touched PLAY and placed the phone on the ground.

Caw!

Without a sound, Lune retreated into the forest and

positioned herself for their northern escape route—three hundred feet to the northeast of Sky and Okeanos.

Silence filled the night as Lune's phone made its three-minute journey to Sky's recorded voice. Then, once again, in the far distance, the caw of a second crow broke the silence.

Caw!

Tunet touched STOP on his cell phone.

Caw!

He touched PLAY and put his phone in the thicket just below his feet.

Caw!

Without a sound, Tunet retreated into the forest, positioning himself next to Lune.

As the recordings rolled on, everyone was in the perfect position for their escape, except Trasnet. Loch and his men had unknowingly trapped him from the others.

Six hundred feet to the east, Sky's recorded voice shouted, "Loch, *ana huna*. Loch, I'm here."

LOCH TURNED TO THE east and yelled, "Do you remember what happened less than an hour before?" He stopped and tugged at his crotch. "Now, it's my time to even the score!"

SIX HUNDRED FEET TO the northeast, Sky answered Loch's call even louder, "Loch, *ana huna*. Loch, I'm here."

LOCH COCKED HIS HEAD from side to side as he scanned the dark shadows of the eastern edge of Great Stag Forest. A stillness fell over the land as he signed to his men, *Stay*. Quickly, he moved to the northeast. If it were not for the clanking of the hooves that dangled from his wrists and ankles, there would be silence.

Clank.

Loch's eyes bulged through the great stag's eye sockets as he moved toward the voice.

Clank. Clank. Clank.

He stopped.

Clank.

Slowly, he moved to an opening in the forest.

Clank. Clank. Clank.

He stopped again.

Clank.

Loch stepped to the side of a gigantic tree and peered deep into the eastern edge of Great Stag Forest—never looking west. Had he looked west, he would have had a clear view of Sky and Okeanos, who were watching his every move from just sixty feet away.

He raised his spear high as he looked to the northeast. "Here's to your death on this night...oh, what joy. Oh, such delight."

He let out another long, sinister howl as he looked up to the night sky. Then, silence befell him.

The Full Moon ridiculed, "Oh come on, Loch. Stop with the chatter. Do you think all your chanting really matters? Think about what has happened. First, she's way over here. Next, she's way over there. How could she possibly be doing this all alone? The Tainted Ones, with their clever tactics, are going to take over the world, and you'll be overthrown. Looks like you'll have to get your own ice...wouldn't that be nice. Now, stop the bantering and look around...before you're the one who's found and bound."

Enraged, Loch glared at his men and signed, *Scatter about. Find them. Bind them. And then let out a shout.*

Finally, Loch looked west and couldn't believe who he saw.

"Nock—" Sky whispered to herself as she placed the arrow on the bowstring.

Loch's eyes locked with hers.

"Draw—" She pulled the arrow back and aimed.

Loch drew back his spear, despite knowing the distance to his target was too far.

"Loose—" She released the arrow.

"Bullseye," Hoppy whispered.

Loch looked down to his right. Her flying spear had pierced his gown, pinning his dominant arm to the tree.

"Nock—"

Sky looked straight into Loch's eyes.

"Draw—"

She aimed.

"Loose—"

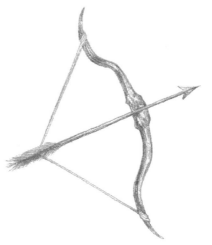

"Bullseye," Hoppy whispered.

Sky's second arrow pierced Loch's cloak, just under his left arm.

"Nock—"

Loch couldn't believe she had pinned him to the tree. Rage ran through his veins—pulsing through his body, bulging in his neck, drumming in his temples. He glared at his guards. "What are you doing, you idiots? Don't you see her standing there? I command you to bind her to anything, anywhere."

"Draw—"

Loch glared over his shoulder at his guards and hissed, "I'll remember the hesitation I see in your eyes. I warn you, defying me would be very unwise."

"Loose—"

As Loch looked up, his protruding eyes crossed as he watched the flying spear pierce the base of his antlers.

"Bullseye," Hoppy whispered.

Loch was pinned to the tree, like a scarecrow. His adrenaline flowed thick, pumped by his fury. He yanked and pulled, but the arrows held him tight.

From her escape position, Lune yelled, "Run, Trasnet!"

The guards smiled at one another. "Trasnet lives?"

Stupefied, Loch glared at his guards as he tried to loosen the arrows' hold. "How dare you defy me! Without me, where would you be?"

Trasnet stepped out of the darkness.

The guards gasped, "Trasnet lives!"

Trasnet said, "Loch, we do not want to hurt anyone, but we demand our freedom."

The guards looked at each other as they thought about what Trasnet had just said.

"Trasnet, your people will never see their freedom day," Loch said as he wrenched his body, trying to free himself. He looked at his guards and commanded, "Kill Trasnet!"

"No," the sorting guard said. "We will not kill Trasnet."

Loch twisted with all his might and glared at the sorting guard. He looked up to the evergreen canopy before snapping his head back hard. "You're a traitor, just like the Medicine Man. May the devil rest the soul of that backstabbing, double-crossing madman."

IN THE DISTANCE, LUNE gasped as tears flooded her eyes. She slumped forward and looked down at the Medicine Man's clothes. *He gave his life for me,* she thought as tears fell to the ground where they were shattered and torn.

ANGRY, THE GUARDS BACKED away from Loch. "You killed the Medicine Man?"

"I put my spear right through his neck. There was a stream of blood, not just a speck," Loch bragged as he freed his left arm.

The guards shook their heads in disbelief. "You're a monster."

QUIETLY, SKY AND OKEANOS moved out of Loch's line of sight. They could see his anger build as he glared at his retreating men.

Suddenly, Loch snapped his head and stared at Lune.

Sky whispered, "Why has Lune moved into plain sight? We were all going to escape now."

Hoppy whispered, "I think she has a battle wound—the deep, down-inside kind."

Had Okeanos known how to use Sky's bow, he would've ended Loch's life right then and there, but he had no weapon of his own and his daughter was in terrible danger. Okeanos signed, *I will go help Lune. You stay here. Trasnet will be with you soon.*

A moment seemed like eternity as two things happened.

"Arghh!" Loch tugged at the arrows with all his might. He was nearly free.

Lune looked up to the heavens and felt the Medicine Man's love shine over her. Once again she became the Great Gray Wolf. At that moment, she blended into her surroundings.

32

GRANDPA DOC

THE LITTLE NOTE ESCAPED the oak door's hold just as Grandpa Doc grabbed it, read it, shoved it in his pocket, and ran to the house to get his medical backpack. *Minutes are hours,* he thought as he raced to the house.

FIVE MINUTES LATER, GRANDPA Doc wrestled the little note from his pocket, shined his flashlight on it, turned the knob of the oak door, and commanded, *"Door Unlock."*

He slammed the door, grabbed the phone, and dialed zero.

The metal door slid quietly from the wall, locking him in.

"I'd like to make a ten-minute call to Lune." He shoved the little note into his pocket.

"This is operator five-one-zero-three-seven. I'm placing the sixth call to Lune at destination coordinates 43 degrees north, 2 degrees east. Please hold while I confirm a connection."

"*Bonjour, c'est l'opérateur quatre-deux-huit-six-zéro. Vous êtes connecté,*" the second operator said.

Grandpa Doc recognized both voices immediately.

"You have thirty seconds to deposit five cents for a ten-minute connection," the first operator said. "The potting shed will return to the origin when the time expires."

Angry, Grandpa Doc asked, "Mom, who is Lune?"

"Lune is the oldest genetically-verified female in my lineage. Sky requested a call to one of her great-grandmothers. Lune's grandfather—who is called Medicine Man—is the oldest genetically-verified male in my lineage, followed by her father, Okeanos. The males named Trasnet and Tunet are Lune's cousins."

"Oldest genetically-verified…what does that mean?"

"Lune is the oldest known female in your lineage. She lives fifty thousand years ago. You have ten seconds remaining to make a deposit."

"You created a time machine! Why are you counting calls?" He forced a nickel into the jar labeled *Deposit*.

"I'm counting calls because the maximum number of calls to a person is six."

"Six!" He gasped. "This is call six!"

Grandpa Doc's concern was lost on deaf ears, as the thirty seconds had expired.

The operator warned, "At the destination, open and close the door using the commands *Open Door* and *Close Door*. At the origin, lock and unlock the door using the commands *Door Lock* and *Door Unlock*. When you're outside the potting shed, keep the door closed. Please take a watch from the watch box. Your ten-minute call will end when the time expires."

Grandpa Doc saw Sky's handwritten note with the commands on the dusty shelf and stuffed it in his pocket where he felt the baggie and its note. "Oh, great, I forgot to hang the baggie up—no one will ever know what happened to us."

He took a watch and shook his head, shaking the anger out. "This watch has the same fancy script as my watch. I wonder if Stella embedded the same technology in it." He turned it over, saw the touchpad surrounding the face, and pressed it.

Poof!

Crash!

Grandpa Doc's body slammed against the metal walls of the potting shed. He peeled his face off the dusty metal wall. "Of course, Stella would make her time machine invincible. I have ten hours to find Sky and get back here."

As the phone went dead, he commanded the door to open. He stepped out of the time machine and into a bitter cold forest. He drew his parka hood tight.

He looked around and saw nothing.

"*Close Door*," he commanded.

As loud as he could, he yelled, "Sky? Sky, where are you?"

33

THE BATTLE

GRANDPA DOC'S WORDS ECHOED through the night, "Sky? Sky, where are you?"

"Loch, *ana huna*. Loch, I'm here." Lune's abandoned phone's recording had just expired.

"Sky? Is that you?"

"Loch, *ana huna*. Loch, I'm here." Tunet's abandoned phone's recording had just expired.

Confused, Grandpa Doc scanned the forest and yelled, "Sky, where are you?"

HAUNTED BY THE FOREIGN words, Loch's guards signed to one another, *Nothing good will come of this. Let's get out of here.*

REAL OR MAGIC?

TRASNET LOOKED THROUGH THE dark shadows of the forest. In the far distance, he saw a great tree—another magical tree—next to Lune. He looked back at Loch, who was nearly free.

LUNE, OKEANOS, AND TUNET were at Grandpa Doc's side within seconds. They signed to him, *Quiet. There's Sky. Follow us.* Swiftly, they crossed the forest. Soon, Grandpa Doc was leaps and bounds ahead of them.

SKY WHISPERED TO HOPPY, "Grandpa Doc found our note!" Instinctively, she stepped out from her hiding place, wanting to run to him.

LOCH'S RAGE SKYROCKETED WHEN he heard the foreign voice. With the rush of adrenaline, his strength increased exponentially as he pulled at the last arrow and freed himself.

"Loch," Trasnet yelled, "I'm here."

Loch laughed as he bellowed, "Trasnet, you're too far to throw your spear." He turned toward Sky and hissed, "But the one I really want…is oh so near." He charged Sky, hurling his spear at her.

Trembling inside the backpack pocket, Hoppy screamed, "Look, Sky!"

Sky let out a blood-curdling scream and jumped behind the tree as Loch's spear whizzed by, barely missing her. Then, she felt his hot breath roll down the back of her neck, sending chills down her spine. A moment later, she felt the crushing pain of his grip as he spun her around.

"Let go of me," she screamed, thrusting her knee toward his groin.

For a split second, she felt his grip loosen. She ran.

Loch's anger raged as he scooped up his spear and quickly stalked her. Finally, he saw the shadow of her bow.

The Full Moon sneered, "You need to end this now. Trasnet is nearly upon you on the left, and Lune to your right."

Intense pain coursed through Sky's body as Loch threw her to the ground—her legs pinned by one of his feet, her head spinning from the blow. She saw Loch raise his spear high above her throat. She turned her head to the side, just wanting it to be over.

"Engage him, Sky!" Hoppy yelled. "Remember what we were taught—run, hide, fight. We can't run and we can't hide, so we must fight! Grandpa Doc is almost here. Don't give up!"

Sky opened her eyes and screamed at Loch, "You're a stupid idiot!"

Loch couldn't resist returning her words. "Just like the Medicine Man, you'll meet your fate. With this spear to your throat, it's you who I'll terminate!"

Bam!

Trasnet plowed into Loch, knocking him to the ground. He pulled Sky to her feet, and they raced toward the others.

Furious, Loch stood up. He saw the foreign man running toward Trasnet and Sky. "Three with one shot. Let them all rot." He heaved his massive spear.

Just a few feet from Sky, Grandpa Doc stretched out his arms.

Loch's blood-chilling laugh echoed through the forest as he watched three people—Trasnet, the Prophecy Girl, and the foreign man—converge in the center of his spear's path.

Lune, who was now less than fifteen feet behind Loch, braced her body in a wide forward stance.

Grandpa Doc watched Loch's spear—just inches from them—as he scooped Sky into his arms, driving his body forward, thinking, *The boy who saved Sky will die if I don't do something.*

Lune fully drew back her spear in her right hand with her left hand extended strongly, pointing to her target.

Grandpa Doc wrapped Sky into his hold, forcefully dragging his foot under the boy's feet. He pressed the touchpad on his watch. *Poof!* Instantly, he and Sky were ten feet away.

Lune's spear headed straight for Loch's back. In the distance, she heard the woeful chant of a Burial Ceremony and knew the Powerful Ones were preparing the Medicine Man's body. A tear fell from her eye as she grieved for the Great Gray Wolf and all the others before him. She looked up to the heavens and prayed, *Forgive me. I did not want to take the life of another.*

The force of Grandpa Doc's kick sent Trasnet's legs up where his neck would have been.

Loch watched his spear pierce Trasnet's calf and let out a howl. But the sound of the howl was cut short as he felt something rip through his back and out his chest. He staggered, looking down at the spear that had taken his breath with it. In his last moment, he heard the mournful chant of a Burial Ceremony. As he watched his own blood spill out before him, he searched for the Moon one last time.

Trasnet screamed as he yanked the spear out of his leg. Within moments, everyone was at his side.

Grandpa Doc wrapped his scarf tightly around Trasnet's calf. He gestured to Okeanos, *Carry him. Follow me.*

They followed him toward the Tree That Was Never There.

"*Open Door,*" Sky commanded the metal door to open.

They dodged inside.

"*Close Door,*" Sky said.

And the door sealed shut behind them.

34

TIME EXPIRED

GRANDPA DOC OPENED HIS medical backpack and took out two shiny metal objects: a box and a sheet. With a wave of his hand, the shiny metal sheet become a sleek operating table.

He looked at Trasnet. "I'm going to fix you. To do this, I need to numb your leg. You'll feel a pinch that might hurt a little—it'll help if you hold Lune's hand and squeeze it. But try not to flinch."

Trasnet nodded.

Grandpa Doc said to Okeanos, "Put the boy on the table on his belly. Hold him still."

Trasnet translated for Okeanos.

"There are pieces of wood, stone, and feather that I need to remove." Grandpa Doc opened the metal box. Inside, his medical tools were neatly arranged. Before he put on his magnifying glasses, he looked at Sky—who was holding Hoppy for dear life—and the others. He thought, *Emotional healing takes time—months, sometimes years. Keeping people busy is one way to help them heal.*

"Okeanos, you're doing a great job of keeping Trasnet still. Keep holding Trasnet's hand, Lune. Hoppy, you comfort Lune. The healing powers of touch and love are amazing."

Grandpa Doc looked at Sky and Tunet. "Sky, please get a watch from the box and scrub up—you can be my assistant. Tunet, you can be my second pair of eyes."

"Time?"

Sky looked at her watch. "Nine hours until time expires."

Grandpa Doc began removing the foreign objects from Trasnet's calf.

TEARS STREAMED FROM LUNE'S eyes, rushing over Hoppy as she clutched him in her arm. When the tears stopped, Lune's voice trembled as she whispered, "I can't believe the Medicine Man is dead."

"I'm so sorry, Lune."

"It's my fault he died. He should've never changed clothes with me. He should've never taken my place in jail."

"Some things—like freedom—are so important that they're worth dying for. Tell me about the Medicine Man."

Immediately, the sparkle returned to Lune's eyes as she told Hoppy all about the man who had taken care of her since she could remember—comforting her when her mother died and entertaining her while her father and brothers toiled in the ice fields.

"We would get up early in the morning and walk all over the countryside looking for medicinal herbs, nuts, seeds, roots, and barks." Lune hugged the little bunny as she relived all her memories. "We believe that when your parent or grandparent go to the heavens, they live on through their children and grandchildren. I wish he had been my grandfather so that he could live on in me."

"I'm positive he lives on in you."

Lune nodded and smiled. "I think so too. I felt his presence and love rush over me during the battle. And I feel it now."

"TIME?" GRANDPA DOC ASKED.

Sky checked her watch. "Five hours until time expires."

"Tunet, did I get all the little pieces of wood?"

"Yes, sir."

"Will you stitch it shut now?" Sky asked.

"No."

"No?" Sky raised her eyebrows. "Are we taking him home to fix him?"

"That would be a good option, but we can't take anyone home and we can never come back. The operator was counting calls, and we reached the maximum calls to Lune. Only you, Hoppy, and I will be returning home." He changed his bloody surgical gloves for a clean pair and pointed out the two silver wands in his medical box. He raised both hands in the air.

Poof!

Just like magic, the wands appeared in his hands.

"Real or magic?" he said with a twinkle in his eye as everyone gasped.

Grandpa Doc knitted the wands just above the wound on Trasnet's leg. "These medical wands accelerate the healing process. The white blood cells already devoured any bacteria or pathogens that infiltrated Trasnet's body through this big cut. Now, it's time to speed up muscle and skin regeneration. Normally, this would take months, but we should be done within an hour or two."

"WOW, TRASNET'S LEG LOOKS perfect."

"Real or magic?" Grandpa Doc said. He helped Trasnet roll onto his back and said, "Keep resting."

"Real! Everything is real," Sky said as she twirled around. "One day, I'll figure out the secret behind your magic."

"Well, you did figure out the secret behind the potting shed. I tried and tried to get that door to open when I was a kid, but you figured it out."

"Tell me the magic behind the healing wands," she begged.

"I honestly don't know how they work. Stella gave them to me as a gift when I graduated from medical school."

"I bet she brought them from the future," Hoppy said.

"I bet you're right, Hoppy." Sky turned to Grandpa Doc. "Stella was from thousands of years in the future."

"Really?" Grandpa Doc squinted his eyes as a million childhood memories ran through his mind. He laughed. "Maybe that's why she always referred to our modern inventions as *ancient artifacts*."

"That's how Stella had the technology to create everything," Hoppy said.

"Who is Stella?" Lune asked.

Proudly, Sky said, "Stella is my great-grandma. She invented lots of things, like this time machine that brought us to you and the magic coin that turns into fireworks." She was almost bragging now. "You should see her observatory—the telescope and workshop are amazing. I'm going to have a desk right next to hers."

Grandpa Doc saw Lune look down, knowing that she wanted Stella and Sky to be part of her life too. He cleared his throat and looked at Lune. "Lune, Stella is one of your many great, great—too many greats to say—grandchildren. We are all family."

Sky scrunched up her face and crossed her arms. "How do you know that?"

Hoppy butted in. "He probably asked the operator."

"I asked Stella—I mean, the operator—and she told me that you had asked to call one of your great-grandmas on your first call. The time-machine's code selected Lune because she's the oldest genetically-verified female in our lineage. The Medicine Man, Lune's grandfather, is the oldest genetically-verified man in our lineage. Okeanos is the next oldest male. Trasnet and Tunet are Lune's cousins."

"The Medicine Man is my grandfather?" Lune gasped as she looked at her father. "Why didn't you tell me he was my grandfather? Why did he live with the Powerful Ones and not us?"

Okeanos looked deep into Lune's eyes. "Loch forced him to live with them because of his medicinal powers. And, Loch, being as crazy as he was, forced us to keep it a secret from you, holding the threat of killing you over everyone's head. Loch did allow the Medicine Man to care for you as a grandfather would…probably because he knew the Medicine Man would be very uncooperative if he didn't."

Grandpa Doc checked his watch. "We have three hours until time expires."

"WHAT'S UP THERE?" TRASNET asked, pointing to the small button outlined by a large square in ceiling. "There must be something—the Magic Tree is as big as any tree in Great Stag Forest or Wild Bear Woods."

Everybody craned their necks, looking at the small *Press* button in the dusty ceiling.

Sky broke the silence. "Hoppy, I remember seeing that button on our first call, but I forgot all about it. I don't have anything long enough to get to it."

Hoppy looked around the room and noticed a long stick camouflaged against the dusty metal walls. "Look!"

Before Grandpa Doc could stop her, Sky grabbed the stick and pressed the button.

The metal plate slid into the ceiling, and a staircase spiraled down.

Trasnet jumped off the operating table. And, with the wave of a hand, Grandpa Doc collapsed the operating table back into a small metal sheet, just as the stairs came to a stop in the middle of the dusty floor. Before he could stop them, the kids ran up the stairs.

Grandpa Doc looked at Okeanos, smiled, and checked the time. "After you."

Sky yelled down to Grandpa Doc, "Wow, the second floor is so much bigger than down there. Wait 'til you see Stella's library." The kids peered at the books, fireplace, and comfortable chairs encased behind the glass wall.

Just as Grandpa Doc and Okeanos reached the second floor, the kids were climbing the stairs to the third floor.

"There's a kitchen and bathroom. Just think of the places we'll go, Grandpa Doc."

The kids raced up the spiral staircase.

"The fourth and fifth floors each have two bedrooms," Sky shouted as they raced to the top floor.

"Jiminy Cricket, it's the command center and an observatory."

The kids ran their hands along the glass wall that encased the command center. Then, they gazed up at the telescope and ladder that were suspended under a glass dome.

"Look, there are hundreds and hundreds of...." Sky scrunched her face up and turned to Hoppy. "Hoppy, what are those called?"

"They're called Rolodexes. Each card in the Rolodex has a person's personal information. The cards are attached to a spindle. There were lots of them on the dusty shelves at Ye Olde Antique Shoppe." For a moment, his heart ached, remembering his years of battle against loneliness and his life behind the cellophane window.

"Rolo what?"

"Rolodexes." Hoppy brushed away the memory.

Sky yelled down to Grandpa Doc, "There are hundreds and hundreds of Rolodexes on a vertical pulley system...and the Rolodex that's engaged is labeled *Relatives* and the card reads *Lune*." She pressed her face against the glass case.

"Hurry, Grandpa Doc. I see all the settings—there's an old elevator control panel labeled *Maximum Calls*. The six is pressed. All we need to do is push a higher number, and then we can come back to visit." She grabbed Lune's hands and twirled around in joy.

Grandpa Doc raced to the top floor. "Sky, don't touch anything."

"Don't worry, everything is in a glass box, like the observatory at home. I haven't found the button to open it yet."

As soon as Grandpa Doc stepped into the control center, Sky jumped into his arms.

"Real or magic, Grandpa Doc?"

Grandpa Doc laughed as he checked the time. "One hour left."

Hoppy, who was still clutched in Lune's arms, said, "The time machine fits inside the potting shed at home...the potting shed isn't this tall. I think we should head back down before it folds into one story." He shivered just thinking about it.

"You're right, Hoppy," Sky said, wriggling out of her grandfather's arms. She took the little bunny from Lune and held him tight as the light from the rising sun streamed through the glass dome and bounced from one glass wall to another before finding its way down the spiral staircase. She looked around the room at all her new friends and whispered to Hoppy, "Grandpa Doc is right—out of most battles, something wonderful happens that would have never happened otherwise. I'm glad Mama and Papa won the battle on moving to the farm."

Sky looked down at her watch and then back up at Lune, Trasnet, and Tunet. "It's time to go home now." She scrunched up her face to stop the flow of tears, but it didn't work. The tears fell like rain.

EXHAUSTED, SKY, HOPPY, AND Grandpa Doc nodded off in a corner of the dusty room. They woke to two clicks of the potting shed door at the exact same time as the metal interior door slid into the wall, exposing the old, oak door. The stopwatch hand pointed to the fancy *Time Expired*.

FIVE MONTHS LATER, THE thorny thicket had grown over the potting shed. A blanket of blackberries covered both *Do Not Enter* signs and the new padlock.

"We're ready for the spaceship's windshield," Papa said. He hammered the last nail into the cockpit where Hoppy was testing out the copilot seat. "Can you run and get it, Sky? It's in the barn, just behind the stack of boxes, near the workbench."

"Sure, Papa. We'll be right back. C'mon, Hoppy." Sky grabbed Hoppy and took off running for the barn.

As she ran past the potting shed, she saw her sword on the ground and heard the roar of the golden-horned dragon. Without stopping, she swooped up the sword and, in one continuous arc, drew it up and over her head as she pivoted into a backward lunge. The sword was within striking distance of the dragon's neck.

"En garde!"

Fire flicked from the dragon's mouth, circling Sky's sword.

"I know what yu' protectin' inside yur castle!"

Flames flew out the dragon's mouth as it thrust its head at her.

"Don't yu' dare let anyone into me castle." And with that, Sky threw the sword into the air and ran like the wind to the barn.

SKY SHINED HER FLASHLIGHT around the barn. "Hoppy, it's really dark in here."

There were neatly stacked shelves here and organized wooden crates there and an old staircase leading to the haybarn upstairs.

"It really is just a barn, right?" Hoppy's voice trembled.

"Of course, it's just a barn." She held him tight.

Hoppy trembled. "You know, Sky, things aren't always what they seem."

"No, you're right, Hoppy. They aren't." She looked around the barn and then spied a dusty, glass box that was big enough to fit a whole person inside. "Look at that, Hoppy."

She swiped the dust off the top with her palm, and they peered in.

"Look, a real double-edged, long sword...and a massive, leather-bound, drawing book titled *History of Dragons: The Highly Intelligent, Magical Creatures*. This book is just like Stella's book in the observatory. Look at all the tabs. I bet the book is hers. And the sword is the same as the two mounted above the fireplace. I'm going to ask Grandpa Doc to teach me how to wield a real sword. Oh, Hoppy, I have to find the button to open this case." She scanned the wall.

Hoppy shook off his fear. "Maybe you should cover the box back up with dust, so no one finds our treasure."

"Good idea, Hoppy." Sky picked up a handful of dust from the floor and blew it on the glass box. "We'll come back here later. Right now, we need to find the spaceship's windshield. I'm sure the workbench is over there. Yes, there it is."

She shined the flashlight behind the crates. "Look, Hoppy, there's the windshield. I just need to move some of these boxes." She lifted the top box and set it on the workbench.

Just as Sky started to lift the second box, she saw a label that read *Ancient Artifacts*.

Hoppy shivered. "Please don't open that box. Let's just get the windshield and go finish our spaceship."

"Oh, Hoppy, it's just a box. Let's just take a little peek."

Real or Magic?

Made in the USA
Monee, IL
01 August 2021